MIND FIELDS

Visit us at www.boldstrokesbooks.com

MIND FIELDS

by

Dylan Madrid

LIBERTY
EDITION

A Division of Bold Strokes Books

2013

This Trade Paperback Original Is Published By
Bold Strokes Books, Inc.
P.O. Box 249
Valley Falls, NY 12185

First Edition: September 2013

Credits
Editors: Greg Herren and Stacia Seaman
Production Design: Stacia Seaman
Cover Design by Sheri (graphicartist2020@hotmail.com)

Acknowledgments

Mind Fields could not have happened without Cindy Cresap, Greg Herren, Len Barot, Sheri, and Stacia Seaman.

For their never-ending support and words of encouragement, I offer my deepest gratitude to:

Albert Magaña, Andrea Patten, Bethany Hidden-Cauley, Cathy Moreno, Cyndi Lopez, Donna Cummings, Elizabeth Warren, Frankie Hernandez, Heather Brant, January Cummings, Jessica Moreno, Joyce Luzader, Keshia Whitmore-Govers, Kimberly Greenberg, Lesléa Newman, Linda Wread-Barnes, Maire Gardner, Marisa Villegas, Michelle Boman Harris, Mindy Morgan, Nance Haxton, Nick A. Moreno, Nita Manley, Patricia Abbott-Dinsmore, Rena Mason, Robyn Colburn, Sabra Rahel, Sal Meza, Selena Ambush, Stacy Scranton, Stefani Deoul, Stephanie Gomez, Susan Madden, Tara Henry, Therease Logan, Trish DeBaun, Todd Wylie, and Vanessa Menendez.

Cyndi Lauper and Nancy Sinatra for songs that made this novel sing.

My parents, Samuel Barnes Jr. and Nancy Nickle, and my brothers, Jamin, Jason, Andy, and Jaren, for allowing me to be the writer in the family.

My colleagues in the brief-residency Master of Fine Arts Writing Program at Spalding University, for sharing their words and creative lives with me.

My students, for teaching me more on a daily basis than I could ever dream of teaching them.

Mike S. for teaching me the difference between right and wrong without even realizing it.

The loving memory of my grandmother, Dorothy Helen Nickle, for my childhood of soap operas and tea parties.

Edward C. Ortiz, for the wonderful life and love we share.

The beautiful people I have lost who still resonate in every word I write.

The city of Chicago, my urban muse that never fails me.

To God, for everything.

For Edward.
For making my dreams his own.

CHAPTER ONE

M oney changes everything.
Those words were printed across the top of the ridiculous poster tacked to a wood-paneled wall inside the lobby of the century-old bank. At the bottom in an equally obnoxious script: *Open a savings account today!* There was a glossy photo of strangers pretending to be a family between the two phrases, betrayed by the forced expression of love on their faces. Their affection for one another was just as fake as the cheap backdrop of a city park behind them.

Actors, thought Adam. *They're no family.*

The father was pretty, clean-shaven, and probably gay.

The mother looked lost. She was petite, Asian, and wearing way too much lipstick for a day out in the sun with her loved ones.

Maybe she stumbled onto the photo shoot by accident, the photographer thought she had the right look, and she landed the gig without even trying. Poor thing.

The child looked Middle Eastern and terribly unhappy, probably forced against his will to hold the melting rainbow-colored snow cone in his hand. His lips were stained with food coloring and his gaze aimed away from the camera, like a loud noise had occurred at the moment the photo was taken.

The three of them looked like hostages, begging to be rescued and taken home.

Adam moved away from the sun-faded poster, took a few steps to his left and pushed open the half-closed, dark wooden door to his mother's new office.

Wow. I'm impressed. Dear old Mom's moving up in the world.

Becca Parsh was sitting behind a computer in an outdated navy blue skirt suit, a broad-shouldered blazer with shiny gold buttons, a string of inherited pearls, and a new salmon-colored blouse that made her look like a politician's dutiful wife. Her blond highlights were in desperate need of a touch-up and she was wearing too much blush and mascara.

As usual, she looked exhausted and overwhelmed.

"I come bearing salad," Adam offered, raising the overstuffed, overpriced plastic container he held, like the lunch was a token of friendship.

His mother pointed to her earlobe and mouthed familiar words: *I'm on the phone.*

Adam nodded, placed the salad in the center of her already-cluttered desk, and started to leave. He moved backward in the same direction he'd entered, retreating toward the doorway and the lobby of the bank. It was a game left over from his childhood that they called *Rewind.* The object was to determine who could move in reverse the longest.

Adam always won. Becca usually fell.

Adam had one foot out the door when his mother held up an index finger and stopped him in his tracks. He gave her a look, hoping for more instructions. She pointed to the empty black leather and chrome chair on the opposite side of her desk. Adam took a seat.

He waited.

He listened.

"Sir, I'm sorry you're upset," his mother said into the illuminated earpiece. The stress the conversation was causing could be heard in her strained voice. Adam knew the tone well, as he often caused it. She was trying to be polite, but frustration was breaking through. She leaned back in her chair and rubbed her temples. "And I understand why. Really, I do. These are hard times for everyone."

You're telling me. At least you have a job, Mom.

Adam's attention shifted. There were three helium-filled balloons trying to free themselves from the streams of pink and yellow ribbons they were secured to. They were drifting like shiny ghosts behind Becca's head, caught in the gentle flow of warm air streaming out of the vent in the ceiling above them. One of the balloons offered *Congratulations!* The other was a maniacal happy face. The third was an odd choice: pictures of a baby's bottle and a pacifier.

Mother, is there something I should know?

Adam grinned at the thought of his forty-year-old mother announcing she was pregnant. Sure, women her age had babies all the time. But if she did, Adam's society-concerned grandmother would never recover from the shock and public humiliation. It was bad enough Becca never remarried, living the lonely life of a widow for all these years, but to commit the ultimate social sin of getting knocked up while unmarried?

That would throw the uptight old broad right over the edge.

Nana would literally die of embarrassment.

"I'll look into the foreclosure," his mother promised the

caller. "You have my word, sir. If the bank made a mistake, I'll make it my personal mission to find it. I really wish there was more I could do for you right now."

Seconds later, she was off the phone. She let out a sigh that was way too heavy for a newly promoted loan officer. She whipped off the wireless headset and started rummaging through desk drawers, frustrated.

"Can I help?" Adam asked.

"I'm looking for a fork," she said to the pile of papers on her desk.

Adam reached into a sweatshirt pocket and produced a black plastic fork, encased in a see-through wrapper. "For the lady," he said, reaching across the desk.

"I don't feel like a lady today."

"But you got flowers," he said, noticing the red vase of white carnations on the edge of the desk. "And balloons. Speaking of which…anything you want to tell me?"

"They're from my promotion," she said. "You know that. I texted you this morning."

"I think I left my cell in Stacey's car," he explained. "Did your text mention anything about a baby shower?"

"What are you talking about?" she asked. Adam pointed. His mother turned to the reflective Mylar faces of the balloons behind her.

"I get the congratulations and the scary-looking happy face," Adam said. "But the other balloon? Should I be concerned? I enjoy being an only child."

Becca's mood lightened. Her face relaxed. "They're from Marge. She's the senior teller. Emphasis on *senior*. It's quite possible she thinks I got promoted and pregnant in the same week. She's confused."

"I want her to wait on me from now on."

"You better hurry," his mother said. "She's about to retire. Next Tuesday, I think."

Adam grinned, amused by his thoughts as he often was. "Maybe she's the pregnant one."

Becca popped open the plastic to-go container. "Thank you for the salad," she said. "I'm starving."

"I wanted to do more," he said. "I know how long you've wanted this promotion."

"This is perfect." She took a bite.

"Once I find a job, I'll take you to dinner. Somewhere worthy of a celebration."

Becca swallowed and said, "That's fine, but I'm paying. How's Friday night? Bring Stacey. Bring Victor."

"Fine. Have it your way. We're college students. And we're broke. We won't argue."

"You usually don't when I foot the bill."

"I have a question," he said. "Who designs those obnoxious posters in the lobby? Your marketing team should be fired. Have you seen those things?"

Becca raised an eyebrow. "Should the bank hire you instead?"

"Only if they know what's good for them," he replied. "Let them know I graduate in June. My rates will triple then. I'm already in huge demand. They're looking at a three-year wait, minimum. But since I completely support all forms of nepotism and I'm flat-ass broke and I blew my only chance at a decent internship, I'm willing to make an exception."

"I'll mention it to Marge," Becca said. "She's in charge of the…décor. I think she's in charge of everything, actually. I don't know what everyone will do when she's gone."

Adam stood up. He had homework to do and a boring

history class to attend later. Then maybe cheap drinks and half-priced appetizers with Stacey and Victor, if they could scrounge up enough cash to hit their favorite happy hour spot.

Chicago is no place to be an unemployed college student. There's so much the three of us want to do we can never afford.

Adam started to move backward.

Rewind.

His mother's words stopped him. "Do you like the office?"

He nodded. "It's twice the size of your old one," he said. "But you need a secretary."

"I have one. Her name is Mindy. She called in sick this morning. I think she puked while we were on the phone."

Adam smiled again and met his mother's eyes from across the room. "My advice?" he said. "Save the baby balloon for her."

Becca grinned. "You're probably right. She's been obsessed with a guy she met on the L train a few weeks ago. I think it's serious."

"Sounds like it," Adam agreed.

Becca's tone changed. She was approaching a new topic of conversation with caution. "Speaking of which, any news?"

Adam appreciated his mother's attempt to show some interest in his nonexistent love life. "Are we talking about subways? Or men?" he asked.

His mother shook the plastic fork at him, a gentle reprimand. "You're too clever, Adam. You have a smart-ass comment for everything. Men don't always like that. It doesn't matter if they're gay or straight."

When did my mother become an expert on the dating do's and don'ts of gay men? Is she writing an advice column on the side I don't know about?

Adam folded his arms across his chest. He'd been working out more lately. He wondered if his mother could tell. Could anyone? Even Victor hadn't mentioned it, and he noticed everything. "Perhaps I need to dumb myself down, then," he said.

"You just need to meet someone who's as intelligent as you," Becca said. "And that won't be easy. You need to get out more. Talk to people. Make yourself available. Or do the right thing and elope with Victor. You know I adore him."

"But he doesn't like me," Adam said. "At least not like that. You know what I mean. We're just friends. Besides, he's too good for me. He needs someone…nicer."

"You're out of your mind," she said. "The two of you are perfect for each other. Once you stop acting like an idiot and you show Victor the sweet boy I know you really are, everything will work."

"Any particular reason why you've suddenly become determined to marry me off?"

She didn't hesitate. "You're lonely."

Adam gave her a look of mock shock. "No, I'm not."

"Don't lie," she said. "I'm your mother."

"Don't tell anyone."

"That you're lonely or that we're related?"

He shrugged. "It depends on who's asking."

She poked at her salad with the tip of her fork. "I don't like what college is doing to you. You're more arrogant than anyone I know who's twice your age. You haven't earned it yet."

"I think you're right," he said. "And twenty-two is too young to be this jaded."

"Enjoy your youth," she reminded him. "I'd kill to be twenty-two again."

"What were you doing then?"

She looked into his eyes with fondness. "I was raising a sassy four-year-old."

"Gee, I wonder whatever became of him," Adam said.

"You might like him," she said. "He's gay and single. He thinks he knows it all and he's too thin for his own good, but he's definitely a catch."

Adam shook his head. "No, thanks. He sounds like an asshole."

Becca smiled. "An asshole wouldn't bring lunch to his mother."

"Yes, but clearly he's forgotten a napkin and something to drink."

Becca opened a bottom desk drawer and pulled out a purse. She fished out a few bills and placed them in the palm of her son's outstretched hand. "There's a vending machine down the hall," she said. "Pretty please?"

"I know where the machine is. I've done this before," he reminded her.

"While you're at it, get something for yourself," she said.

"Your promotion has made you generous," he noted. "I can't wait for Christmas this year."

"This doesn't mean I'm paying your cell phone bill again this month, so don't ask."

"Do you treat all your minions like this, Lady Loan Officer?" he asked.

"Only the ones who refuse to find a job," she replied.

"Why bother?" he asked. "I thought you were marrying me off. I'm assuming he's wealthy. My job will be to keep him happy and spend loads of money and organize charity events. Just like a *Real Housewife*."

Becca let out a small laugh. "Don't count on it," she said.

"You expect me to play stupid for a guy with no cash? Next thing I know, you'll be convincing me love makes the world go round and to go with my heart. What has this promotion done to you? Where is my mother? What have you done with her?"

"I'll tell you everything I know for a cold pop and a napkin," she said. "And hurry. There's a gallon of vinaigrette on this salad and half of it's on my face."

"How classy we are," he said, before leaving by walking backward out of the office and returning to the lobby.

Once he was out of his mother's line of vision he turned face forward, ending the current one-player round of *Rewind*.

Another victory for me.

Adam passed by the obnoxious *Money changes everything* poster that had caught his attention just moments earlier. This time, he didn't give it a second glance. Instead, he focused on his mission.

Sierra Mist for Mom. Diet Pepsi for me. I know the drill.

He stopped in front of the vending machine and aimed a dollar bill at the thin mouth. He caught a quick glimpse of his somewhat distorted reflection in the transparent plastic face of the machine.

Mom's right. I'm too thin. I don't want to be a jock or anything lame like that. That's not my style. Never will be.

I'm cool with being the nerdy college guy. But still, some tone and definition would be nice. Is that too much to ask for?

Adam's gaze moved farther, past his own features and to the somewhat grimy black and white checkered floor behind him.

Seeing the square tiles triggered a childhood memory. His grandfather was there in the long hallway, standing by the silver drinking fountain like a protective bird. The old guy was wearing his favorite Irish tweed cap and black and yellow bowling shirt. He hadn't shaved in a few days and looked like he needed a shot of whiskey.

Adam was six. Maybe seven. Together, they were waiting for his mother to close her teller window and join them for the all-too-important task of going shopping for school clothes. The errand had to be completed during her lunch hour. Since Mom's car was in need of some expensive repairs, Grandpa offered to drive.

Adam had kept himself occupied by playing a solo game of hopscotch, jumping on alternating legs and feet from one square to the next. Each time, he landed with a catlike grace. He loved the echoing sound his rubber-soled blue and white sneakers created when they made contact with the marble floor. He was completely immersed in the activity until he heard his grandfather clear his dry throat and say with concern, "What're you doing, Adam?"

I looked up at him. I remember that moment. The look on his face, in his eyes. Couldn't he tell? Why did he have to ask? It was obvious.

"Boys don't play hopscotch," his grandfather explained, shaking his head with slight disapproval.

"But I'm good at it, Grandpa," he replied. "So why shouldn't I do it?"

They locked eyes, sharing a brief and silent conversation. Finally, Grandpa retreated. "I suppose you're right. There're a lot worse things you could do."

I wondered if he knew then. Did he know in that very second his grandson was gay? That hopscotch was just the beginning?

Adam slid the first bill into the vending machine and pressed a button. The purchased soda slid down an internal tunnel and landed with a thud. He repeated the process.

He bent down and retrieved the two cans, welcoming the sting of the cold aluminum against his palms. He clutched the sodas tightly, heading back in the direction of his mother's new domain.

As he walked, Adam felt temptation tickle the back of his neck. He struggled for a few seconds, resisting the sudden impulse.

Don't do it. People will think you're strange.

As he neared the end of the hallway, he broke into an impromptu game of hopscotch in clear view of the customer-filled lobby. The stares and smiles coming at him from all directions only urged him on. He reached the final black square and took a bow, despite the absence of applause.

"You're the type of person people can't ignore," his best friend Stacey had told him after they'd known each other for only a week. They were sitting in what was now their favorite Irish pub, in a wooden booth soon to become their usual spot, toasting their new friendship by tossing back shots of watered-down tequila.

"You've got it all wrong," Adam said. "I'm the one who's always overlooked. The last one picked for the team."

Stacey shook her head. "No," she said. "Seriously, you walk into a room—any room—and people stop and stare at you because you take their breath away."

Adam smiled and laughed. "I never realized I was so attractive," he replied, half-joking.

"You're not," she said, dead serious. "It's not about that. Not at all. I think you were just born with it."

"An irresistible charm?" he asked, still hoping for a compliment.

"Gravity," she explained. "You pull people toward you, Adam. It's very powerful and you don't even realize it. I love to just stand there and watch it happen."

He stared into her eyes. "Is it happening now?"

"No," she said, refusing to look away. "It doesn't really work on me. I think I'm immune to it. From what I can tell, it has the strongest effect on men."

"What are you smoking, Stacey?" he said. "Men don't notice me."

"Bullshit," said Stacey. "Maybe it's *you* who's not aware."

In the bank lobby, Adam whizzed past the poster of the fake family and filled the open doorway of his mother's office with his strong presence, like an actor making a grand entrance at the top of the second act.

"I'm back, by popular demand," he announced, followed by: "Oh, sorry."

They were no longer alone. There was a tall man standing in Becca's office. Adam zeroed in on the back of the stranger's head, on his thick, dark hair and sun-kissed neck.

The man had a physical response to Adam's voice. It was evident in the way his shoulder blades tensed and the muscles in his back tightened. Like someone had surprised him with a touch, or a kiss.

Adam's gaze moved across the back of the older man's body in an involuntary sweep, performing a quick study of his every inch: the way the short sleeves of his maroon golf shirt hugged his biceps and how his khakis fit his buttocks perfectly.

The stranger turned around. Adam tightened his grip on the cold cans, hoping they'd somehow cool the hot flash he felt creeping into his face. Surely this stranger could tell Adam's attraction to him was immediate and severe.

Look away. He can tell you think he's hot. Stop checking him out.

With just one glance, the older man stripped away all of Adam's confidence and left him feeling nervous and intimidated, strangely awkward and unsure of himself.

Just leave. Don't say a word. Rewind.

Becca stood up. The back of her office chair got entangled with the three balloons behind her.

Is it my imagination, or is he checking me out, too? Damn. I think he is. And my mother saw him do it. How embarrassing.

One of the balloons—the crazed happy face—broke free and floated up toward the ceiling. It brushed against the overhead fluorescent light fixture. The contact caused the bulb to flicker and the balloon to pop, a muffled gunshot sound. Adam and Becca flinched, startled. The stranger didn't flinch, didn't react at all. He paid no attention to anything at all.

Anything except Adam.

"Dario Vassalo, this is my son," Becca said. "This is Adam."

Adam felt the man's gaze drift over his body, taking him in and devouring him alive. He repeated Adam's name in a deep, take-charge voice that seemed to fill the space between them and resonated with masculinity. He took a step toward Adam, who nearly dropped both sodas. The man took the aluminum cans from Adam, allowing his fingers to brush gently against Adam's skin. "You may call me Dario," he said, but Adam wasn't sure to whom his words were directed.

"Hello," was all he could manage to say.

Dario Vassalo placed the cans of soda on the edge of the cluttered desk, next to the red vase of white flowers. He looked at Becca, smiled, and then returned his attention to the office doorway.

"I didn't know you had a son," he said. "I didn't know you were old enough."

Becca seemed flustered, too. Adam could see the heat in his mother's cheeks beneath the layers of blush. She looked out of place standing behind her desk, like she'd been caught doing something wrong or was somewhere she wasn't supposed to be. He could tell she was nervous because she didn't seem to know what to do with her hands.

Adam glanced at the sleeve of his mother's blazer, noticing the fresh grease stain near the cuff. He lifted his eyes to her mouth. The smudge of the oily salad dressing was gone and her lipstick was slightly smeared.

I forgot to get her a napkin. Poor thing had to use her sleeve. I'm definitely going to hear about this later.

"Mr. Vassalo," she breathed, "you say the nicest things."

The man's eyes stayed on Adam. "I believe in speaking my mind," he said.

Adam licked his dry lips, swallowed, and spoke. The sound of his own voice surprised him. "So do I," he said.

Dario raised an eyebrow. "Excellent," he said. "I had a feeling we had something in common."

What in the hell is happening here? This man has to

be twice my age, if not more. He looks like someone who plays tennis with James Bond, drives a sports car, and dates supermodels. And I think he's Italian or Greek or something Mediterranean—which is probably why he's so fucking hot.

"Adam is in college," Becca offered. "He graduates in June."

"What are you studying?" Dario asked.

Sex. Wanna help me with my homework? I could write one hell of a research paper about you.

Adam's gaze darted between his fidgety mother and the intoxicating Dario Vassalo. "I'm double majoring," he said, "in English and marketing."

"He wants to be a copywriter," Becca said. "And he's good at it."

"I'm sure being a copywriter is a lot more interesting than building subdivisions," Dario said with a smile.

Adam stayed close to the doorway, ready to leave. "I wouldn't know," he replied.

"It's terribly tedious work," the man continued, "but it pays the bills, as they say."

"I'm sure it does," Adam said, eyeing Dario's expensive watch, inhaling his strong cologne, making note of his manicured hands—and his wedding ring.

This guy screams first class. What's he doing talking to us?

Adam saw Dario glance down at the open container of soggy salad. "Did I interrupt lunch?" he asked.

Adam watched his mother as she closed the plastic lid and said, "It can wait."

"I won't keep you long," Dario promised. "I'm here to discuss your proposal."

"I won't lie to you, Mr. Vassalo," she said, avoiding his

eyes. "Today is my first day on the job, so to speak. I was promoted last week."

"Congratulations," he said with a small nod of approval.

"So the proposal is very important, as you can imagine."

"I've been in business for many years now," he reminded her. "I know what it means to a financial institution to become our preferred lender."

Slowly, Becca sat back down in her chair and said, "I see."

"I also know how important my business would be to a newly promoted loan officer," he said. "Especially one I find so…charming."

This guy's laying it on super thick, but he's no fool. My mother is eating this up. She won't need lunch by the time he leaves.

Dario glanced back to Adam and returned his focus to Becca. "I'm sure we can figure something out," he said. "That's what negotiations are for."

Becca gestured to the empty chair across from her desk and said, with borderline flirtation, "I'm ready to listen if you're ready to talk."

And I'm ready to leave.

"It was very nice meeting you," Adam said, stepping into the hallway.

Dario's voice stopped him in his tracks. "I'm sure we'll be seeing each other again," he said.

Adam felt his skin reignite, a direct result of Dario's attention. "I look forward to it."

Adam didn't say good-bye to his mother. He moved away and stood just outside the office for a moment to catch his breath and regain his composure.

The conversation between his mother and her hot new client continued. Adam listened, but only for a few moments.

"Your son," Dario began. "You say he's studying English and marketing?"

"Yes," Becca said. "He's a senior at DePaul."

"I'm impressed," he said. "Any job prospects?"

"Not in the near future," she said. "There was a possibility of an internship."

"And?" Dario prompted.

"Let's just say Adam doesn't interview very well."

"This is really none of my business, but how he is supporting himself?"

Becca took a breath before she spoke. "He gets a modest check every month from the government. My husband was in the military. He was killed in the line of duty."

"Oh, I'm very sorry to hear that."

"It's all right," she said. "It happened a long time ago. In fact, Adam never had the chance to meet his father."

"You raised him alone?"

"With the help of my husband's family," she explained. "Especially Adam's grandfather. We never would've survived without him."

Adam moved away from his mother's office, leaving the conversation behind as quickly as he could. He'd heard enough. He was certain his mother would succeed, the sexy stranger would make more money to add to his fortune, and Adam would still be unemployed and struggling to get by living off the meager benefits of a man he'd never met.

He stopped for a moment when the badly designed poster caught his eye again. This time, he pulled the tacks out of all four corners, rolled the thing up, and tucked it under his arm.

Adam moved to the revolving door exit.

I'll put it up in my room so I can see it every day. So I'll know what never to do as copywriter.

So I can constantly remind myself: money changes everything.

CHAPTER TWO

"It was kind of embarrassing, if you want to know the truth," Adam told Stacey. They were sitting in their usual booth at the low-lit Irish pub two blocks away from the overpriced apartment they shared. "I think it was obvious he was checking me out. I'm sure my mom noticed."

Adam was on his second cider. Stacey was almost drunk.

Her style of the week was 60s retro. With a slicked-back dark ponytail, knee-high boots, a vinyl miniskirt, and a barely-there blouse, she looked like a go-go dancer from some classic dance TV show.

Or a really expensive hooker.

Adam smiled at the thought.

"My mother would've paid the guy to take me out," Stacey said on cue, as if she had the ability to read Adam's mind. "Or blackmailed him into marrying me."

"I think he's already married," Adam said, reaching into a bowl of stale pretzels.

"Are you serious? Was he wearing a ring?"

He nodded. "He was. It was nothing fancy, but it was there."

Stacey slammed the gouged surface of the table with

her palm. "Holy shit! You get hit on by a hot married guy while I'm stuck getting eye-raped by rednecks at a rodeo boutique. Whose life am I living?"

Adam laughed. "No offense, but I'll take mine over yours any day."

Her fire faded. "Yeah," she said, "so would I. I need to find another job. I hate working retail."

The mood at their table shifted. Stacey lowered her eyes. Adam realized one of her false eyelashes was crooked.

"You look sad now, Stacey," he said. "Did I make you sad?"

"No," she said, "I think I'm sober."

"How? You've already killed three ales and two shots of tequila."

"Tolerance," she said. "I have too much now."

He shook his head in mock disapproval. "That's what happens when you drink six nights a week."

She gave a slight shrug. "I needed a hobby," she said. "And I suck at bowling."

"Try shopping. My grandmother can teach you."

Stacey shook her head. "No way. That woman terrifies me."

"That says something. You don't scare easy."

"Speaking of fear," she said. "The rent is due."

Adam pushed the pretzel bowl away. "God, don't remind me. Wait," he said. "I thought we weren't allowed to talk about serious stuff when we come here."

"Who said?"

"*You* did. It was your rule."

"Fair enough. No more mentioning married men or bounced checks. Don't hate me for saying this, but I think I need to drink more." She scanned the bar. "Where's Victor?

He's a college graduate. Maybe he's feeling generous. Didn't he get a temp job last week?"

"What's the occasion? I mean, other than the fact you're alive and breathing."

Her posture relaxed. She was a marionette whose strings had been cut. "I'm lonely, Adam."

"Join the club."

"What are you talking about? You've got Victor."

Adam leaned back in the booth, pressing his shoulders against the wood. "I don't *have* Victor."

"Oh my God, you *so* do."

"No," Adam said. "You're delusional."

"He's totally your fall-back guy. He's obsessed with you, which means if things don't work out with someone else, you know in the back of your twisted mind Victor will be there."

"You've completely lost it," he said. "Please tell me you're huffing paint on the side."

"I can't afford it."

"And I'm here to tell you Victor and I are just friends. We always will be. Nothing more. He's just an awesome guy I met in German class who likes to hang out with us a lot."

"Does he know that?" she asked. "Have you broken the news to the lovesick man? Or will you admit you like it? All that attention and devotion. Maybe it makes you feel better about yourself…just a little?"

"Is this a therapy session or happy hour?" he asked.

"Probably both. You know how we are," she said.

"He's very sweet."

"Sweet?" she repeated. "What is he? A cupcake?"

"No, I think he's adorable," Adam admitted. "Maybe

in another life it would work out between us. In this one, he deserves much better than me."

"Finally. The truth. It's only taken three years."

"I'm not dumb, Stacey."

"Just because you'll be graduating summa cum laude doesn't make you a fucking expert on love," she said,

"Who said anything about love?"

"You did."

"No, I didn't."

"It's the look on your face whenever you talk about him," she said. "I can see it in your eyes. You can't hide that."

"Clearly you need to drink more," he said.

"Bullshit," she said. "Look at him."

"Why?"

"To prove my point, asshole."

Adam glanced over to where Victor stood on the opposite side of the pub, staring intently at the face of a dartboard with an arm raised and poised.

"Let's go back to *adorable*," Stacey said. "What else do you see?"

"A guy who's really good at playing darts."

"He's got good aim," she said. "I'll give you that. What else?"

"What? You want like an essay? An ode to Victor? Since he's Mexican, would you like my term paper in Spanish, as well?"

"Can you try not to be a smart-ass for one conversation?"

"You've been texting with my mother again. She said almost those exact words to me earlier today. A coincidence? I don't think so. The two of you have formed a conspiracy against me. I have no proof, of course, but give me time."

"Um, can we stick to one topic? Please, Señor Paranoid?"

"I don't know what you want me to tell you."

"How 'bout what you see when you look at him? You have to admit he's cute."

"I thought I already said that."

"No," she said. "You told me he was *adorable*. That's not the same thing as *cute*."

Adam avoided Stacey's eyes. "I've never really looked at him that way," he said, not really sure why he was lying. The truth was he'd been attracted to Victor since the moment they met. Yet for some reason, Adam felt the need to keep those feelings in check.

"Well, why the hell not? God knows he looks at you like you're his favorite combo platter."

"Did you really just say that?" he asked. "Was that a reference to his weight? What a cheap shot."

"Is *that* what this about?" she said. "Are you really *that* shallow, Adam Parsh? Please tell me you're not. Victor isn't fat."

"Well, he's not thin either," he said. "Not that it matters to me, of course. But you know how men are."

"Nice save," she said. "Tell yourself whatever you want, but we both know you can be a real jerk sometimes."

"I agree with you," he said. "Victor isn't fat."

"Just because you look borderline anorexic and never have to work out—"

"Don't judge."

"Practice what you preach, my friend. Victor is stocky."

Adam almost laughed. "Stocky?"

"Husky," she said. "I think he's hot."

"Are you describing a man or a vegetable?"

"I'm talking about the love of your life," she said. "Only you're too stupid to know it yet."

Stacey scooted out of the booth. It took her a second to steady herself on her feet.

"Where are you going?" Adam asked.

"To ask our stocky, adorable Mexican friend if he'll buy me another drink," she said. "In the meantime, you sit here and think about what you've done."

"What exactly am I guilty of?"

"I don't know, but if you figure it out while I'm gone, let me know when I get back," she said.

Stacey stumbled off. Seconds later Victor was catching her by the arm to save her from falling flat on her inebriated ass.

They were too far away and the pub was too loud to hear their conversation, but Adam imagined it went something like:

"Oh my God, Victor. I think you just saved my life."

"Are you okay, Stacey? You need to be more careful. You could've gotten really hurt."

"No chance of that happening with you here to protect me."

"Me?"

"Yes, *you*! I always feel safe with you around. Like you'll take care of me no matter what. Adam feels the same way. He says so all the time."

"Well, of course I will. Isn't that what friends are for?"

"Absolutely! I think we should celebrate our friendship tonight. Let's have a drink!"

"Okay, but I'm buying."

"Awwww, you don't have to do that."

"I insist."

"God, Victor you are *so* sweet."

Whatever she said to him, it worked. Within seconds, Stacey had a cocktail in her hand. She'd moved on to seducing the uninterested tattooed bartender. Having served his purpose, Victor was now a mere afterthought.

Poor guy. He never stands a chance against Stacey. She wins every time.

❖

Meeting Victor Maldonado felt like destiny. Adam was certain something big and powerful had a hand in how the moment played out. It was beyond sheer coincidence: it had to have been orchestrated, arranged by some invisible force determined to make sure their paths crossed and their lives merged. Their friendship fell into place with instant ease, becoming something the other had been missing but never realized it until the moment they said *hello.* Finding Victor in the middle of a sea of self-absorbed strangers at school felt like a blessing to Adam. Sure, he had Stacey, but he wanted something more. He wanted to feel a connection with someone he'd never experienced before.

Adam wanted to fall in love.

Their worlds collided on the first day of German class three years ago in a third-floor classroom at a community college in downtown Chicago. Victor happened to take the empty seat behind Adam's desk. Adam happened to have forgotten something to write with.

Later, they'd frequently remember the moment with laughter, relishing it like a delicious inside joke. In the retelling, Victor would most likely remind Adam that forgetting something to write with was a now a frequent occurrence, a bad habit.

"I should've known it would be the first of many pens you'd steal from me," Victor would say while the happy memory was still lingering in the nostalgic air between them.

Adam would smile and maybe laugh. He'd say, "I think I have all of them in a drawer somewhere."

Victor's voice was soft and often melodic. His words—the very sound of them—would add tenderness to the moment with a variation of: "I've suspected this all along. You're holding them for ransom, aren't you?"

They would lock eyes, speaking inside the words they both were dying to hear but that were always muted by their mutual trepidations. "I should give them back to you on your fortieth birthday or something cool like that."

"No," Victor would say. His smile would disintegrate and a serious expression would fill his sorrowful eyes. The hopeful words would slip right out of his heart. "You should save them for our wedding day."

Adam would shake his head, dismissing the moment as something to make him smile or maybe laugh at. Even though he could see the truth in Victor's eyes, he avoided it. He never allowed their conversations to stray too far down that road, always steering clear of uncomfortable territory.

Defining their relationship became a constant thread in their conversations. What were they to each other? Friends? Potential lovers? Soul mates?

"Our friendship is strange," Victor said one night when they were waiting for the L train. They were standing on the platform of the Belmont Avenue station. It was snowing. Adam was shivering.

"I know," Adam agreed.

"What are we to each other?" Victor asked.

"We're best friends," Adam said. "You know that."

"Nothing more?"

"What do you mean?"

"How do you describe the…perfectness between us? I know you feel it, too."

Adam was thankful the train arrived at that moment, pulling into the station with a rumble and squeak loud enough to kill the conversation.

Since then, they'd both kept it safe, always disguising their strange connection with humor. They would poke fun at the fact they both knew Victor was crazy about Adam and admitting it wasn't going to happen—although Adam really felt the same way. Victor developed the ability to slip into their every conversation some sort of gentle reminder that he was *there*, constantly floating and drifting around the outer edges of Adam's universe, just waiting for the spoken invitation to enter his orbit.

In the beginning, they struggled through German class together. That was their link, their common ground. Through late-night studying sessions and flash-card drills, a bond was created, sealing their friendship permanently. They complained about how strict the professor was, speculating if Frau Lehmann had a love life or was just a sexless spinster. They dissected the odd behavior of strange classmates, wondering who was carrying the deepest, darkest secret. They passed notes to each other that included phrases like *Just kill me now* and *I like that color on you*.

It didn't take long for Adam to figure out Victor's feelings for him extended beyond just friendship. It was soon apparent in the frequent surprises that showed up, usually at the precise moment when they were needed or craved. Like the iced white chocolate mocha Victor would often carry into class, somehow knowing it was Adam's favorite, remembering it from some sliver of a conversation they'd had.

"How did you know?" Adam asked the first few times it happened.

Victor always gave him a look of surprise. "You told me."

Adam's gaze would drift off as if he were searching a nearby wall for the words to their past conversation, the transcript of what had been originally said. "I don't remember telling you that."

"That's what I'm here for."

"To remind me of the things I forget?"

"Yes. And to bring you coffee every morning."

"You're too nice to me. You don't have to do that, Victor."

"I know," he said. "But I like to."

Adam would ask the question, already knowing the answer. But he did it because he loved to hear Victor say the words. "But why?"

And there it was: "Because it makes you happy."

Once the semester came to an end and German class was done, they started meeting at sidewalk cafés. This lasted for a few weeks until the weather got cold and they eventually found themselves sitting side by side in dark art-house movie theaters watching classic German films. Adam could always sense Victor's eyes on him. Sure enough, every time he would turn to look at Victor, his friend was staring at him instead of the images on the screen.

"Why are you staring at me?" Adam asked with a grin. "Am I that interesting?"

"You are," Victor said. "You make me dream."

To celebrate hitting the one-year mark in their friendship, they took the L train to a German neighborhood in Chicago called Lincoln Square. They bought spicy meat and sweet cheese and fresh baked bread at a German deli there. They sat on a bench near a *closed for the season* fountain sharing the food, dreaming aloud about what it would be like to run away someday to Europe.

"Would you go with me?" Victor dared to ask.

"To Europe?"

"Anywhere?"

Adam nodded. "I would."

"You would?" Victor sounded surprised.

"Of course I would. Aside from Stacey, you're my best friend."

"Will I still be your best friend when we get married?"

Adam looked away. "You don't wanna marry me, Victor."

"What if I do?"

"You'll just end up hating me."

"Never," Victor vowed. "So, would you consider it? Spending the rest of your life with me?"

Adam laughed to lighten the mood. As usual, he hated it when things got too intense. When that sweet desperation crept into Victor's beautiful dark brown eyes, Adam was instantly filled with an intense wash of guilt. He became cautious with every word he spoke, fearing he'd crack Victor's fragile heart. The last thing he wanted to do was cause his best friend any pain. "It might complicate our new lives in Paris."

As if it were an unspoken rule between them, Victor seemed to pick up on the subtle warning signs Adam gave, indicating Victor had pushed the subject of their possible romantic future too far. Adam was grateful Victor knew how and when to back off. Victor steered them back to a less intimate level, out of the danger zone and back to safety. "You'd pick Paris over Berlin?"

"I'd pick Paris over anything," Adam said.

"Then Paris it is. Besides, there's an amazing art school there I've always wanted to go to. Maybe I'll apply. I can learn to sculpt like Camille Claudel."

Victor tossed the last bit of bread crumbs to a flock of nearby pigeons before he started to pack up their things. He wrapped the meat in butcher paper and the cheese in wax paper and placed them in his backpack, struggling with the stubborn zipper. Adam reached out and touched Victor's sweatshirt sleeve, causing him to freeze in his movements.

"But promise me if you meet someone and you fall madly in love with him, you and I will still be friends," Adam said.

It was Victor's turn to look away, as if the thought were too unbearable for him to consider. "You have my word."

Later that same day, they stumbled upon a German street festival called Oktoberfest. Amidst the high-spirited crowd, traditional music, and heavy air that smelled of yeast and bratwurst, Adam and Victor indulged. They drank too much beer, puked in an alley behind the train station, and staggered back to Adam's apartment. They passed out side by side, sprawled across Adam's bed, only to wake in each other's arms just before dawn. At first, both were captured by the tenderness of the moment, the sweet feeling of belonging to someone. They were drawn to the warmth of skin, the familiar scent of one another. But when Adam felt the softness of Victor's lips brush lightly across his cheek, reality kicked in and set off a round of panic. Adam pulled away, rolling over to face the window. He focused on the light blanket of fresh snow drifting by, heading down to the city street below. He tried to ignore the sigh of disappointment that slid out from Victor. Adam had woken aroused. He battled with the temptation to turn over and let Victor touch him. He longed for the pleasure but knew if he gave in, it could ruin everything between them.

And that's what he feared the most.

Adam knew Victor was a great guy. He was cute in a boy-next-door way. Sure, he was a little heavier than most and rarely hit the gym, but he was true to his word, a diehard romantic, and somewhat obsessed with Adam.

Adam often wondered why Victor was so enamored with him. He didn't think he was particularly attractive. Usually, Adam felt invisible and plain. He'd gotten used to being the boring guy men never gave a second glance to. But Victor's constant attention made him feel good about himself. It made him feel beautiful and desirable.

Thoughts of Victor plagued Adam, keeping him up most nights or distracting him throughout the day.

What would happen to their beautiful friendship if they crossed the intimate line? Would Victor still feel the same level of intensity? Or would his devotion and interest be diminished and eventually disappear?

What's my problem? Everyone seems to think Victor's the greatest guy in the world and perfect for me. Clearly, I'm attracted to him. Why I am not jumping in and taking a leap of faith?

Adam knew the answer, and occasionally he needed to remind himself of it, to keep everything in perspective.

Because Victor deserves someone better.

❖

Adam caught Victor's eye from across the emptying pub. Happy hour was coming to an end.

Adam offered him a smile. Victor blushed a little, lowered his dark brown eyes out of shyness, and slowly moved to the edge of the table where Adam sat alone.

"May I join you?" he asked.

Adam nodded. "Of course."

Victor slid into the empty seat, took a sip from his bottle of his Guinness, and licked his lips. "Stacey seems to be having a good time."

Adam glanced over to where his dark-haired roommate was perched on a bar stool, batting her fake lashes at unsuspecting strangers. "She always does," he said.

"What about you?" Victor asked.

Adam looked at Victor. Beneath the warm glow emanating from the simple light fixture hanging above the table, Victor was radiating with endearing naïveté. Adam struggled with the impulse to lean across the wooden surface and kiss him, putting an end to the three-year torture he'd subjected them to, once and for all.

"What about me?" Adam said. "What do you mean?"

"Are you having a good time?" Victor asked. He seemed genuinely concerned. He always was. Adam had lost count of how many times Victor had put everyone else before his own needs and wants. How much more could a guy do or sacrifice to prove his love?

Dive in. Step off the ledge. Tell Victor you think everyone is right and you're a complete fuckup for not listening to them sooner. Look him in the eye and tell him you know deep in your heart the two of you were meant to be together. Give destiny a chance, you asshole. There will never be another man in your life like Victor. And you know it.

Adam took a breath and said, "I always do when I'm with you."

The words stayed suspended in the air before sinking in and filling Victor's heart. Adam could see it in his eyes: the realization that maybe Adam had finally come to his senses. That divided lines were going to be crossed soon, ridiculous barriers would finally get knocked down—maybe even tonight. Adam knew Victor couldn't ignore the promise in his words, the more inclusive newness in his tone.

Victor swallowed and said, "Oh yeah?"

Adam nodded and smiled. Then he slid a hand across the tabletop and grazed a fingertip gently over the top of Victor's knuckles. "Later, will you help me take Stacey home?" he asked.

Victor looked confused and unsure. He gripped his bottle of Guinness so hard, Adam wondered if it would shatter. "Of course," he said. "Don't I always?"

"We could watch a movie or something."

"Sure," he said. "Whatever you want is cool with me."

Adam knew he had to take the conversation one step further, to make sure Victor really knew what was about to happen between them.

How can I tell this guy what I'm feeling? God, he looks so freakin' adorable right now just sitting there with all kinds of hope and love in his eyes. Why did I make him wait so long?

Adam decided to swim deeper. "Then maybe…well, I was wondering…maybe you could spend the night."

Victor's eyes widened. He pulled his hands away and placed them in his lap. "Spend the night?" he repeated, unable to hide how nervous he'd become.

"Yes," Adam said. "With me."

Victor lowered his gaze. "On the couch?" he said. "Like usual?"

Adam smiled and shook his head. He felt like he was seeing Victor for the very first time. He was allowing himself to finally recognize the incredible beauty in him—the dark hair, the full lips, the innocent eyes.

I've been such an idiot for so long. How lucky am I this wonderful guy stuck around and put up with my bullshit for three years? Don't let him change his mind and give up on me now.

"No," Adam said. "In my bed. Next to me. Where you belong."

Victor raised his eyes and looked at Adam. "Is that what you want?" he asked. "And be honest. Because you know how strong my feelings are for you."

Adam reached for the bottle in front of him, tilted his head back, and drained the last few drops of cider. He wiped his wet mouth with the back of his hand and said, "Victor, you are everything to me."

CHAPTER THREE

The silence was awkward and new. They were sitting on the couch as they had so many, many times before, but tonight they were farther apart than usual.

Adam felt nervous and didn't know why.

Well, this sucks. Now he's afraid of me. Or I'm afraid of him. We're acting weird with each other. I don't like this.

Like the rest of the apartment, the living room was too small. The old plaid-patterned sofa barely fit in the space. A coffee table, or even a lamp, was out of the question. A flat-screen TV covered half the wall space, but since Adam and Stacey couldn't afford cable, it was rarely turned on. The room was usually dark, except for a faint fluorescent glow coming from the closet-sized kitchen behind them. The tiny bulb above the stove was always on. Adam kept waiting for the thing to burn out and die, but it was apparently invincible.

I've known Victor for three years. I care about him. Hell, I'm probably madly in love with the guy and it's taken me this long just to figure it out.

Adam glanced over to where Victor sat. He looked

pensive and out of place, like he was either waiting to get painful dental work done or about to be suspended from school by the principal.

Or start a new relationship.

"Are you okay?" Adam asked, finally.

Victor closed his eyes for a second and said, "I think I drank too much."

He wants to go home.

"I thought you only had two beers."

He shrugged. "I didn't eat today."

"Why?" Adam asked.

"New diet," he said. "It's not working."

Adam's eyes drifted over Victor's body, taking him in. "Then don't do it."

Their eyes met then. "Easy for you to say. You can eat whatever you want and get away with it. Not me," he said. "The truth is…I want to be the best possible version of me."

"What for?" Adam said.

Victor didn't look away. "For you."

Adam reached across the empty space between them. His fingers meshed and twined with Victor's. He liked the feel of Victor's skin against his. It was soft and warm. "You're fine just the way you are."

The tension in the room seemed to lessen. Victor's lips curled into a small smile of relief. His shoulders relaxed a little. "Do you really mean that?" he asked.

Adam nodded. "Of course I do."

They weren't technically alone, but Stacey was passed out cold. Victor had practically carried her from the cab and up the three flights of stairs. The toes of her go-go boots had slid across the hardwood floor as Victor half dragged her to the safety of her bedroom like a drunken doll. She'd slipped out of his arms and crash-landed face down on her unmade bed.

"Help me turn her on her side," Victor had instructed.

Adam complied, surprised at how light Stacey was. It was like turning over a piece of paper. "Why are we doing this?"

"In case she pukes," Victor said. "You don't want her to choke."

"You've done this before."

"It's a part-time job."

"I hope she pays you extra on the weekends."

That was twenty minutes ago. Since then, the two young men had been hugging opposite ends of the sofa like the sides of an incredibly deep swimming pool and they couldn't swim, afraid to let go.

Until now.

"Yes," Adam answered. "I mean that."

"So, you're attracted to me?"

"Have I ever given you a reason to believe I'm not?"

"It's been three years," Victor said. "I kinda figured you would've given me some sort of hint or a clue by now. I mean, there's been signs, but…"

"Are you solving a case, Detective Maldonado?"

Victor nodded. "It's definitely a mystery."

"Me and you?"

"All the time that's past," he said. "We've never dated other people. How come?"

"Maybe I didn't want to."

"Well, neither did I. You're all I ever think about."

"I'm scared, Victor," Adam said.

Victor gave him a look. "Of me?"

"Of this," he said. "What we have is so amazing. I don't want it to change."

Victor tightened his grip on Adam's hand. "Do you think it will?" he asked.

"Yes," he said. "That's why I've never let us cross the line before."

"Are you changing your mind?"

"No. Are you?"

"I'm ready to jump over the line," he said. "I'll run across it if you want me to."

"What if we do this and...you don't want me anymore?"

"How can you even say that? Do you really think I'm that kind of guy?"

"I think you're lousy at German and you always have been," said Adam. "But I think you're awesome."

"I think I'm in love with you," Victor said. "No."

"No?"

"No. Fuck that. I *know* I'm in love with you. There's no *maybe* or *possibly*. I am in love with you, Adam Parsh. And we both know it. So, what do you want me to do about it?"

"I want you to shut up," Adam said, "and kiss me."

Adam slid over to Victor's side of the sofa. They hesitated a moment before leaning in to the kiss, to the absolute point of no return. In the second before their lips touched for the very first time, Adam stared deep into Victor's eyes. Any doubt or hesitation was erased. All he could sense was how right the moment felt, how much he'd longed for it to happen but had refused to admit it.

Their mouths met, easy and gentle at first. Then Adam felt Victor's palm pressed lightly against his face, guiding him deeper into the kiss. The moment was overcome by raw urgency. The sensation of Victor's warm breath against his lips made Adam tremble. His body felt like it was on fire, his skin emitting steam and smoke.

A sound startled them both. Adam recognized the ringtone at once. It was his mother, trying to reach him. But where in the hell was the phone?

Victor slid a hand between the sofa cushions. He pulled out the missing cell.

"I'm always losing things," Adam admitted. His words sounded breathless. He took the phone from Victor. "I thought I left it in Stacey's car."

"Are you gonna answer it?" he asked.

Adam shook his head. "I don't want to."

Victor grinned. "I don't want you to either."

Adam stared at his mother's face flashing on the screen of the phone. She always looked guilty in every photograph taken of her. Even when she tried, every picture resembled a three a.m. mug shot. "It might be important."

Victor pulled away. "Then you should answer it."

"Okay." Adam touched the phone with his fingertip and then placed it against his ear. "Mom?"

Adam only half listened to his mother. Clearly, she was excited about something. Adam tried to focus but was distracted by his concern for Victor.

Pay attention to what your mother's saying.

Mr. Vassalo gave her the account. The bank manager was pleased. Were they still on for dinner on Friday night?

Congrats. That's great. Of course.

Adam watched as Victor stood up and moved to the round oak dining table, shoved in a tiny sliver of a space directly behind the sofa. Stacey had found the table on sale at a secondhand store a week after they rented the apartment. She haggled and flirted and bought the thing for next to nothing. They didn't realize one of the armless chairs wobbled until they got it home.

Victor sat down in the sturdier of the two chairs. Adam

noticed something on the table caught Victor's eye. He reached for it, unrolled it. It was the poster Adam had been carrying with him all afternoon and night. The one he'd taken off the wall of the lobby of the bank.

"Money changes everything," Victor read aloud.

Adam knew these words were true for his best friend.

To say Victor grew up poor was an understatement. According to the stories he'd shared in confidence with Adam, his childhood was one big blur of waiting in lines. At the welfare office. At the food pantry at a Catholic church. At the grocery story with an embarrassing food stamp debit card.

When Victor was nine, his father left. Hopped into a souped-up El Dorado and rode his way out of Victor's life forever. Victor was left to take care of his younger brother and sister, and a mother who put being a decent role model for her children at the bottom of her short list of priorities.

Adam knew Victor had tried his best to keep a close eye on his siblings. But once they got their first taste of lust for a wilder life, they were ruined.

When Victor turned eighteen, he made the decision to walk away and leave his family behind. They were on their own now. He was done taking care of them. He cut all ties.

Victor's sister Yvonne got pregnant at fifteen. Less than a year ago, his fourteen-year-old brother Lorenzo was shot five times by a boy a year younger than him. By some strange coincidence, he bled to death on the sidewalk outside the bank Adam's mom worked at.

Breaking away from his family inspired Victor. He enrolled in art classes at the community college where he later met Adam; got an office job; rented a studio apartment with a to-die-for view of Lake Michigan; volunteered at a nearby senior citizen center; and, when he wasn't sculpting, he spent every spare second pursuing Adam.

Wait. Pay attention. Your mother just said something about a job.

Mr. Vassalo was impressed. Wants to hire you to tutor his daughter in English. She wants to be a writer. Interview is tomorrow morning.

Tomorrow? Oh, shit.

"Well, what exactly did he say?" Adam asked his mother. "He did? Are you serious?"

"It's weird," Becca said on the other line. "I get this strange feeling you helped seal the deal today."

"Me?" Adam said. "What did I do?"

"I don't know, but it worked," she said. "I think he was on the fence until you walked in. Maybe he was really impressed by you."

"Maybe," Adam said. "Or maybe he's had a tough time finding a tutor for his daughter."

"Do you need train fare to get there?"

"Is it far? Where is it?"

Moments later, Adam hung up the phone.

He stood up. He went to the dining table and sat down in the wobbly wooden chair.

"I know this sounds crazy," he said, "but I think I just got a job."

Victor raised an eyebrow. "At the bank?"

"No," he said. "I met a man today."

Something inside Victor dimmed. Adam could see it in his eyes. "Wow. That was fast," he said. "How should we break it to the children?"

Adam smiled. Victor always knew when some humor was needed most. "He was in my mom's office when I stopped by there this afternoon," said Adam. "He's some guy who designs houses or engineers subdivisions."

Victor glanced down at the unrolled poster in his hands. Adam noticed the edges were curling inward. "A rich guy?" he asked.

Adam nodded. "Very."

"What does he want with you?" The question felt loaded and Victor's words seemed heavy and tinged with jealousy and concern.

"He wants to give me a job," Adam said.

"Oh yeah? Doing what?"

"Tutoring his kid in English."

"But you don't really like kids."

"Well, I do now."

Victor rolled the poster up. "So when do you start?"

"I have to meet with his wife tomorrow."

"He has a wife?"

Adam cracked a smile. "You sound relieved."

The light started to creep back into Victor's eyes. "I'd be lying if I said I wasn't."

"He's my new boss," Adam reminded them both. "You have nothing to worry about. I don't think anyone or anything in this world could compare to what we have."

Adam meant what he said and hoped Victor believed him. He couldn't tell by the expression on Victor's face, a mixture of sadness and deep concern. The energy between them had shifted when Adam answered the phone. All signs of lust had evaporated into thin air. Now the mood felt awkward again. In the three years of their friendship, Adam couldn't remember the two of them ever feeling so disconnected.

What's happening here? Is he backing out? Did he

really just change his mind because I might have a new job? This makes no sense.

"And I'm happy for you," Victor said. "If we weren't already buzzed I'd suggest going out to celebrate."

Celebrate. I can't remember the last time I did that.

For as long as Adam could remember, life had been one struggle after the next. When he was younger, his mother stressed every month about paying bills, often having to ask for humiliating help from her former in-laws. In high school, Adam soon realized he had very little to compare with his affluent classmates. He took the first job he could get, washing dishes in the low-lit kitchen of an Italian restaurant with dirty walls that shook every time the L train rumbled overhead. Since he'd started college, every penny was accounted for. Sacrifices were made. Fun was missed out on. Chances were lost. Adam had learned at an early age to make the best out of any and every situation.

But love was something entirely different.

Adam knew he had to end the evening. Maybe things between them would feel more normal in the morning. He took a breath before he spoke. "I'm actually kind of sleepy."

Victor's eyes shifted toward the light above the oven as if transfixed by the white glow. "Are you?"

"You look bummed."

"I'm not."

"Yes," Adam said. "You're bummed, Victor. I can tell. You can't lie to me."

"Just a little bummed, maybe. I was hoping we could pick up from where we left off."

"I would…but I have an early morning tomorrow."

"How early?" he asked.

Adam's eyes moved to where a clock should've been hanging on the wall. "Super early."

Victor stood up, almost knocking over his chair. He steadied it with both hands, then dropped to one knee in front of Adam.

He's either going to propose to me or plead his case.

"I could stay over," Victor said. "Drive you there in the morning."

God, Victor has the most incredible eyes. So dark and sad and beautiful. Look away or you'll let him stay.

Adam shifted in the uneven chair. "They live in the suburbs," he said.

"Any particular one?"

Adam hesitated before he said the words. "Lake Bluff."

"Wow," said Victor. "You weren't kidding. The guy *is* rich. Lake Bluff is really far. I don't mind taking you."

"I can just take the Metra. It's no big deal."

"Right," Victor said. He stood up and looked deep into Adam's eyes. "No big deal."

"Trust me," said Adam. "I had no idea this was going to happen."

"But you're happy it did," he said. "I can tell."

"If you're so good at being able to tell when I'm happy, then you should already know I want this to happen," said Adam. "And I'm not talking about the job."

"Us?"

"Yes," he said. "I want there to be an *us*. Nothing's changed."

Victor smiled. Adam was tempted to stand up and kiss him again. Then lead him by the hand to his bedroom, undress him, and explore every inch of his body. But he knew it wasn't the right time. Soon enough.

"You know how much it means to me to hear you say that."

Adam rose to his feet. He leaned in and kissed Victor's cheek. He was reminded of how sweet and tempting the scent of Victor's skin was. "I do," he whispered.

"It's going to kill me to walk out the door and go home," said Victor. "Alone."

"We've waited this long, haven't we?" said Adam.

"So, we're officially postponing tonight?"

Adam nodded. He yawned for effect and said, "But a rain check is guaranteed."

Victor placed his hands on Adam's face. The kiss that followed was just as intense. "Do you promise?" he asked Adam as they pulled away.

"Have I ever gone back on my word before?"

They spoke in silence for a moment. Their eyes were reflecting questions and fears, uncertainties and insecurities that would need to be assured and calmed sooner rather than later.

Victor glanced down at the table. "Hey, where *did* you get this thing?"

Adam grinned. "Isn't it awful? It was hanging up in the lobby in the bank."

Victor seemed surprised. "You took it?" He moved toward the front door of the apartment. He turned the dead bolt, unlocking it.

"Yeah, I took it."

"You stole it from the bank?" Victor laughed. "That makes you a bank robber."

Victor opened the door. A chill moved inside.

"I told you were too good for me," Adam said to the back of Victor's head.

He froze in his steps. Victor turned, looking back at

Adam. At once, the hurt was apparent. It was all over his face. "No, you didn't," he said.

"I didn't?"

"You've never said that to me before."

"Sure, I have. I know I have."

"Maybe you have." Victor shrugged. "But I never took it seriously."

"Well, we both know it's true."

"Do you really think that?"

How did this beautiful night turn so quickly? What did I do wrong? He keeps looking at me like he's going to cry. I never should've said anything. Everything was fine just the way it was.

"I think you're amazing and sexy and sweet," he said.

Victor's voice cracked with emotion. "But?"

"But…maybe you deserve better," he said. "And if you feel differently in the morning, I'll understand. Maybe you don't need a forgetful thief to bring you down."

"I got a problem with that," Victor said. "Because I don't want anybody else but you."

"Maybe you just haven't met the right guy yet."

Victor held Adam's gaze. "Or maybe I have and he's too stupid to know it."

"If I hadn't answered the phone…"

"We'd be halfway to Paris by now."

"Paris? How will we even get there?" Adam asked.

Victor touched Adam's face, just lightly. "You're right."

"I am?"

"About tonight. About Paris. About that stupid poster," he said. "Money changes everything."

Victor turned and headed to the stairs.

Adam closed the door and retreated to the couch. He sat

there for what felt like hours, replaying the entire night in his mind. When he was done, he reached further back to the beginning of his friendship with Victor. He thought about each significant moment, the memories that always left him smiling. All along there had been signs. True feelings were brewing beneath the surface since the moment they'd said hello. Now emotions were finally out in the open. They'd been spoken, declared. There was no turning back. The future seemed perfect.

Adam closed his eyes, begging for sleep to come. Instead, the tiny tickle of worry started to gnaw at him until his entire body ached for relief.

What am I so afraid of?

CHAPTER FOUR

Although the schedule at the Ravenswood Metra station said the commute was only fifty-four minutes, the ride seemed much longer. Adam was seated with a window view, heading north on the Union Pacific line toward Great Lakes, to the wealthy shoreside suburb of Lake Bluff, a place he'd only read about or heard others mention.

It was early, but Adam had made a point of buying a large cup of coffee at 7-Eleven before jumping on the commuter train. The coffee warmed a chill inside him he hadn't been able to shake since waking up.

While Stacey still slept, Adam had stumbled around the tiny apartment, half-asleep and filled with lingering concerns. He showered, dressed, ate a bowl of instant oatmeal, and headed for the train station. He checked his phone more times than usual. No voice mail or text from Victor.

Maybe I should've let him stay last night. I could've woken up in his arms, next to his warm body. We could've made love for hours.

Adam barely noticed the sights as the train continued its journey to the North Shore. Instead, he sipped his coffee, listened to overly sentimental love songs on his iPod, and tried to imagine what life would be like if he and Victor made a commitment to each other. He knew, more than ever, that's what he wanted. Being with Victor made sense. Like so many people had said before, they made a great pair.

Questions and fears heightened Adam's anxiety, racing through his mind. Were they too young to be so serious? To be exclusive? What if Victor decided he was bored and restless and wanted to date other people? What if he was tempted and unfaithful?

His phone buzzed.

Finally.

False alarm. It was only Stacey. *I can't wear my new boots today because it's snowing outside. I hate February. But I love you. Where you be?*

He texted back. *On a train heading north.*

She responded within seconds. *I hope you're not running away from home just because the rent is due.*

He smiled and texted back. *Job interview. Wish me luck. Otherwise it's noodles and tap water for us until March.*

The train was nearly empty now. A young woman wearing a red knit scarf and matching cap was sitting a few seats away. A businessman in a gray suit was reading a newspaper he'd folded in half. He was balancing a leather briefcase on his lap. His black-framed reading glasses looked like they'd slip off the tip of his nose at any second.

I wonder what their lives are like. Is she in love with someone she can't have? Is he unhappy in his marriage? Are they terrified of dying alone someday?

Adam glanced down at the pleated slacks, button-up Oxford, black pea coat, and Italian leather shoes he was wearing. He was dressed like a preppy boarding school student. He felt like an impostor. He'd assumed someone else's identity in Chicago and was now on his way to fool a rich family into believing he was one of them.

They'll see right through me.

Adam wondered why Dario Vassalo had extended the invitation to him. Given they'd only spent a few minutes together in Becca's new office and their conversation had been brief, Adam tried to figure out what it was he'd said or done to inspire the wealthy man to consider him for the tutoring position. Was he replacing someone who'd been fired or quit? Were ulterior motives at work? Was the position created just for Adam as a way for Dario to see him again?

Adam shook his head, dismissing his absurd theories. Yet, in the back of his mind, he knew there was a thread of truth to them. He'd felt an instant heat for Dario, powerful and intense. He was almost certain the attraction was mutual.

Get that ridiculous idea right out of your head. He's a married man. You have Victor now. And you love him. You need the job. If you have to flirt a little to get it and keep it, you're just doing what needs to be done. You can make this situation work for you until graduation. Even if the train ride is forever and these stupid shoes are already killing your feet.

Adam finished his coffee. He looked out the window at the passing neighborhoods, wondering what was happening inside the houses and apartments. Was someone brewing coffee, cracking open eggs, pouring pancake batter over a buttered grill? Was a child running late for school, worried they were going to miss the bus? Did someone decide to call in sick for the day, add another log to the fire, and curl back into bed with a good book and a cup of peppermint tea? Maybe a car wouldn't start. An alarm didn't go off. A husband didn't come home.

The train pulled into the quaint, historic Lake Bluff station. Adam said a silent prayer, stood, and exited. Outside, the biting morning air seemed even colder than it had been in the city. There was a thin mist, floating and mingling with the falling snow flurries.

Adam slid both hands into the pocket of his pea coat, cursing himself for not remembering to wear gloves or a scarf. He moved around the crowd of Chicago-bound commuters waiting to board a southbound train and made his way to the front of the train station.

Adam checked his phone and reread the instructions his mother had texted him.

A cab will be waiting for you at the station. Don't be late.

On the train, Adam worried there'd be so many taxis he wouldn't be able to figure out which was his. He was relieved to see there was only one idling at the curb.

An older woman was standing next to the cab. She was short and squat. She was wearing a purple windbreaker, powder blue polyester slacks, and a pair of blindingly white sneakers. She was also wearing a white visor low on her forehead, just above her eyes. Her hair was short, tightly permed, and had a bluish tint.

She looks like an overgroomed, mean poodle.

She glanced at him, cracked a sunflower seed between her front teeth, and spat the shell out on the sidewalk. "You Adam?" she asked. Her voice was raspy from too many cigarettes, and she had a thick New York accent.

Adam was hesitant. "Yes. That's me."

"Name's Myrtle," she said.

"Myrtle?" Adam repeated, trying to hide his amusement.

No one is really named Myrtle, are they?

"Myrtle Brubaker," she said. "You heard of me before?"

Adam couldn't tell if she was joking.

Myrtle Brubaker had been through some hard times, and it showed on her face. She looked weathered. Beneath her haggard appearance and blotchy red cheeks there was just a trace of the attractive young girl she once was. Adam imagined she spent her nights on a bar stool, shooting the breeze, chain-smoking, and killing off a bottle of bourbon— or two.

"Get in," she instructed. "You don't wanna keep the missus waiting. She's got a busy schedule."

Adam slid into the backseat of the cab. It was like sitting in a closed box of sweet-smelling cigars. He rubbed his eyes, coughed a little, and asked, "What does she do?"

Myrtle found his eyes in the rearview mirror. "Who?"

"The missus," he said, already speaking Myrtle's language. "Mr. Vassalo's wife."

"Name's Evangelina."

"That's pretty," he said.

"Doesn't even do her justice, if you ask me. She's a knock-out. You'd think her husband would pay more attention to her, but what do I know?"

Adam grinned. "You seem to know a lot, Myrtle."

"I love three things in this world," she said.

"Is one of them bourbon?" Adam guessed.

"As a matter of fact it is," she said. "I love bourbon, a good horse race, and Nancy Sinatra." On that note, she turned a knob on the dashboard and Nancy Sinatra's distinctive voice filled the taxi with her song "Bang Bang (My Baby Shot Me Down)."

"I've been working in these parts for almost eight years," she explained.

"Do you live in Lake Bluff?" Adam asked.

She looked at him like he was crazy. "Do I look like I do? Nah. I got a place just north of Great Lakes. Can't be too far from the Navy base. When I'm not helping out the Vassalos, I'm driving drunk sailors home at all hours of the night. They tip me well 'cause they know I'm a lady who keeps her mouth shut." She glanced up at the mirror. "I bet you're the quiet type, too."

Adam shrugged and looked out the window. They pulled away from the train station. "Sometimes," he said.

"You know how to keep a secret. I can tell by looking atcha. Probably why they hired you."

"Actually, I don't have the job yet. It's just an interview. I'm not sure how this even happened. I only met the man for a few minutes," he said. "This was my mother's doing, really. So I don't know anything about secrets."

"You know how these rich families are," Myrtle said. "Always tryin' to hide sumpin' from the world."

Is she testing me? Trying to find out if I gossip? Can I really keep a secret?

"You didn't answer my question," he said, with his eyes still turned toward the window.

"Won't be the first time I forgot whatcha asked me," she said. "I'll be sixty-eight in June."

"Does Mrs. Vassalo work?"

Myrtle nodded. She turned down the radio a little. "She got the raw end of the deal when they moved here from Athens," she said. "Some say she was a big-time doctor over there in Greece."

"She's not anymore?" Adam asked.

"Nah. She works at a hospital not too far from here, but she ain't no doctor," Myrtle explained. "They wouldn't let her practice medicine on account she did all her schoolin' in Greece. I guess they made her a high-paid nurse or sumpin'. I'm sure she'll fill ya in."

"I can't believe how big these houses are."

"You ain't seen nothing yet, kid. This is what we call the poor part of town. Where you're going, it's one of the biggest houses out here. An estate is what they call it. Looks like a castle to me. I bet you'll be lost inside that thing in no time. I know I would be."

"A castle?" he said. "You're joking, right?"

"I dropped a guy off at their house once. He said it was a Tudor mansion. I think he was an architect. Probably works with the mister."

"I don't know much about architecture," Adam said.

"I don't neither," Myrtle replied. "But I know rich people when I see 'em."

"Everyone I know is broke and just trying to get by," Adam said. "It was just my mom and me growing up. My grandpa helped us out a lot."

"What happened to your father? Did he run off? Mine did."

"He died."

In the rearview mirror, Myrtle raised an eyebrow. "Murdered?" she asked.

Adam felt the familiar buzz of his cell phone vibrating in a pocket of his pea coat. "You could say that," he said. "He got killed in the war."

"Oh yeah? Which one?" she asked.

Adam fished out his phone. "The Gulf War," he said. "I never got to meet him. He died right before I was born."

There was a text message from Victor. *Last night was weird and wonderful. Just know I'm always thinking about you. Good luck on the interview today.*

Adam sighed, relieved.

Everything between us is going to be okay. Last night was just a strange fluke. Victor and I will be laughing and back to our old selves again in no time.

"That's a real sad story, kid," Myrtle said. "You want a toothpick to take your mind off it?"

Wait. Maybe Victor's having second thoughts. Maybe he woke up and changed his mind.

"How's a toothpick gonna make me feel better?"

"I got a whole bunch of these things. Cinnamon toothpicks. They burn your tongue so bad you forget about whatever's weighing on yer mind. I got some sunflower seeds if ya want those instead."

Adam shook his head. "I'll pass."

"Well, if ya change your mind, let me know."

"Thanks, Myrtle."

Adam texted a quick message back to Victor. *Almost to the interview. Thank you for the sweet message. Will text you when I'm done.*

Impulsively, he sent a second one. *I'm always thinking about you, too.*

Myrtle made a turn onto a private paved road lined with towering pines. The trees cast a kaleidoscope of shadows over the cab. Their branches hung heavy, blanketed with snow. The cab rounded a corner. Adam took a deep breath, amazed by the view of the massive house.

Sure enough, Myrtle was right. *It does look like a castle. This place is straight out of a movie.*

The cab came to a slow, graceful stop. Adam could hear gravel beneath the wheels.

"Well…here we are," she said. She straightened her white visor and licked her lips.

Adam continued to stare through the backseat window, unable to take his eyes off the impressive sight. "Jesus Christ," he said.

Myrtle chuckled. "I don't think he lives here with 'em, but I'm sure he's got a great view of this place from upstairs."

"I knew Mr. Vassalo was a rich man," Adam said, "but I had no idea he was a millionaire."

"About ten times over," Myrtle said.

"Seriously?"

"Must be nice," she said. "To never hafta worry about money. Know if you want something bad enough, you can just buy it. No questions asked."

"I wouldn't know," Adam said.

"Me neither," she said. "But maybe someday, right? Maybe it'll happen for both of us."

"Maybe," Adam replied. "I don't really think about money very much. Probably because I usually don't have any."

"Ya get in good with these folks, I'm sure they'll take care of ya. Just the kind of people they are."

"I have to get the job first," he said, with his hand on the silver door handle. "It was nice meeting you, Myrtle."

She locked eyes with Adam in the mirror one last time. "We can't say our good-byes just yet," she said. "The missus said you'd only be here for fifteen minutes. Then I'm taking you back to the station."

"Fifteen minutes?" Adam said. "That's it?"

"I suppose she's a good judge of character."

"For my sake, I hope not."

"She has to be," Myrtle said. "Otherwise she wouldn't

ask me to do favors for her like picking folks up from the station. She's got good taste."

A sudden case of nerves washed over Adam. He felt out of place, unsure of himself. Doubt was setting in quickly. *I don't belong here. Look at this place.*

"Do I just walk up to the door and ring the bell?" he asked.

"Jane will let you in," Myrtle explained. "She works for the family. Lives with 'em even. She's a bit moody for my taste but that's just because she's British. You know how they are. All uptight about everything all the time."

"Thank you, Myrtle," he said. He opened the cab door.

"Get in there and get the job," Myrtle said. "You're too skinny. I can tell just by lookin' atcha you're about as broke as I am. You need to eat."

Despite his nerves, Adam managed a small smile. "The rent's due and I think I'm in love with my best friend."

Myrtle nodded and reached for her bag of sunflower seeds. "The rent's always gonna be due," she said. "Now, love, on the other hand...That can be expensive. In more ways than one."

❖

Adam stepped out onto the graveled circular driveway. There was a narrow path bordered on both sides by pristine snow. He followed it to the bottom of the marble steps leading to the arched double doors. He stood there for a moment just gazing up at the house.

Adam took a breath, whispered a silent prayer, and hoped he'd somehow manage to maintain his composure and not embarrass himself.

If anything, this will make for a great story to tell Stacey later over a bottle of cider at the pub. Or tonight when Victor and I can finally resume where we left off.

There were two front doors, side by side. They were arched, wooden, and looked like they were centuries old. Adam's hand was trembling slightly when he reached out and pushed the illuminated doorbell. There was a loud gong-like sound. It resonated through the front of the house.

Seconds later, the door on Adam's left slowly opened. On the other side of it stood a woman in a white button-up blouse and long black skirt. Her gray hair was pulled back out of her face. She looked worn out. He assumed she was Jane.

Her eyes were pale blue, almost silver. She gave Adam a quick inspection, glancing him over from head to toe. "Follow me," she said.

Adam crossed over the threshold and stepped inside. Jane pushed the door closed behind them.

The foyer was exquisite. Adam glanced up to the glittering chandelier. His eyes shifted to the grand staircase.

"Wow," he allowed himself to say.

Jane motioned for him to follow her. Adam obeyed.

This is nothing new to her. She works here. I'm just a nuisance, disrupting her day.

Adam was taken to a formal sitting room with a baby grand piano and another chandelier. He sat down in a red velvet chair in front of a floor-to-ceiling window. The thick green drapes were open and tied back with gold velvet ropes. Through the sheer curtains, he caught a glimpse of Myrtle waiting behind the wheel of the cab. She was singing and smoking her cigar, lost in Nancy Sinatra's voice.

Adam glanced around the room, noticing the family photographs. There was a framed picture of Dario Vassalo on the table next to his chair. The photo had been taken on a yacht. Dario was shirtless. Adam tried to look away, but the photo was too enticing to ignore. He couldn't turn away from Dario's naked torso—the dark chest hair, the erect brown nipples, the tanned olive skin.

"Do you like the photo?" Evangelina Vassalo asked. "It was taken in Santorini last summer."

"I've never been there," he replied.

Evangelina was a striking woman, with intimidating beauty and a commanding presence. Adam stood, fighting the impulse to break into applause or fall at her feet. She was wearing a cream-colored pantsuit and expensive-looking heels. Her hair was thick and dark, shimmering with auburn highlights, spilling down around her shoulders. Her eyes were pale green, similar to the sea in the photo of Dario on the yacht.

She's a living Greek goddess. Her real name is Aphrodite.

"You must be Adam. I'm Evangelina Vassalo." Her voice was deep, seductive, and alluring.

Evangelina extended her hand. It wasn't a friendly gesture. Adam shook her hand and was surprised at how incredibly soft her skin was.

"It's nice to meet you," he said. "This is beautiful… you…your home."

"You're very kind," she said. She had an accent. It wasn't thick but noticeable enough. "And you're just as my husband described you."

Dario described me? How? The poor college student who needs a job in the worst way?

"My daughter is a complicated girl," Evangelina explained. "She wants to be a writer. She says she wants to write mysteries. Can you believe that? She's only twelve."

Adam wasn't sure what to say. "That's wonderful."

I am such an idiot. This woman hates me. She's so classy. And I'm...me.

She folded her arms across her chest and gave him a thorough but quick inspection. "My husband thinks you can help her," she said. The doubt in her voice was impossible to ignore. "Do you think you can?"

Adam looked Evangelina in the eye. "I can certainly try."

She raised an eyebrow. "Do you want to be a writer as well?"

"No," he said. She looked surprised. "Well, sort of. I'm planning on a career in marketing or advertising. As a copywriter."

"I'm not familiar with that phrase. What do they do?"

"They write...copy."

I want to go home now. Back to my apartment. Back to Chicago. My life. Anywhere but here.

"So, then you *do* want to be a writer?"

Adam shrugged. "Sure."

"And you're studying English at the university?"

"Yes. I go to DePaul. I'm graduating in June."

"And then what will you do?"

I have no fucking idea, lady. Backpack through Europe. Drink all night and sleep on a beach all day. Marry Victor Maldonado and run off to Paris with him so he can finally go to that art school he's always talking about. Do you really give a shit about my mediocre life?

Adam was sure Evangelina could tell his smile was forced. "Find a great job," he said. "I hope."

"So we will only be hiring you for a short period of time?"

She sounds pleased. She doesn't want me here. Maybe she even put up a fight, but her husband won this round. She'll agree to the job if she knows I won't be here for very long. So I'll go away and stop bothering her.

"I can definitely be here until June," he assured her.

"That's only five months away. I'm not sure what you can do when you have such little time."

Adam held her stare. "I can try my best."

"And you're willing to travel this far?"

"Yes. To help your daughter, of course."

Her glance moved to a family portrait on the wall near the piano. "Anastasia can be a difficult child."

Hopefully no more difficult than her mother.

"Great," Adam said. "Then we'll get along very well."

"Her father spoils her," she said. "I tell her no. He tells her yes. You must not let her manipulate you."

She sounds like an absolute terror. Between that and the long train ride, is this really worth it? Just for a job? Maybe Victor can hook me up with the temp company he works for. They're always finding him decent office gigs.

"If she does not follow your instructions, you come to me," she said. "I will handle it."

"I'll be honest with you—"

"Mrs. Vassalo."

Adam felt his cheeks burn bright with embarrassment. "Mrs. Vassalo," he said. "I'm not quite sure what's expected of me here. What is the job exactly?"

"It's quite simple," she said with a shrug. "My husband met you. He likes you. He created the position."

So this wasn't her idea? She's not exactly thrilled to meet me.

"It's clear to me you need a job," she went on. "I was in school myself once. I studied for many years. Worked very hard."

Looks to me like it paid off.

"And then I moved to this country."

She's right about one thing: I need this job.

Adam cleared his throat. "Mrs. Vassalo, if your daughter wants to become a writer, she'll need to learn her craft. I can teach her. I can assure you if it's her intention to write mysteries, I can provide her with the tools she'll need to become the very best."

The expression on her face softened just a little. "I see," she said. "I sense you are passionate about the English language. And about teaching."

Adam slipped his hands into his pockets. His fifteen minutes were almost up. He'd be leaving soon and probably not coming back.

"I'm passionate about many things," he said. "Especially my future. Obviously, I'm not from your world. I don't come from much. I grew up in Chicago. In Rogers Park. Lake Bluff is not who I am. But maybe someday it will be. If you decide to give me this opportunity, it will be an excellent learning experience for me…and for Anastasia."

Silence followed. Adam could hear his own heartbeat. He wondered if Evangelina could hear it, too.

Finally, she spoke. "I think I've heard enough, Mr. Parsh," she said. "You start on Monday. At three o'clock. Don't be late."

"I won't be," he said, stunned.

"Oh. And one more thing," she said. "I expect you'll do your best to stay out of my husband's way. He's a very busy man. It's best that you leave him alone."

Evangelina Vassalo turned and walked away, leaving only an invisible trail of her perfume behind.

❖

Adam crawled into the backseat of the cab. He felt hot, sweaty, and thirsty. The car reeked of cigar smoke. He rolled down the window and breathed in the chilly air.

Myrtle pulled away from the house. "What did I tell ya?" she said. "Is she gorgeous or what? It's like talking to a movie star, don'tcha think?"

"She made me nervous," he confessed.

Myrtle nodded. "She does that to everybody. It's her way."

"Even you?" he asked with a grin.

Myrtle laughed. "Especially me," she said. "She's the only woman I've ever met…I can't look her in the eye. I think she's got some kinda magical powers."

"She isn't human," Adam agreed. "She's either a goddess or a superhero."

"I'll go with goddess," Myrtle replied.

Adam's mind went back to the photograph of Dario, and his half-naked body. To the beautiful allure of his skin, his face, his lips. Adam tried to ignore the overwhelming pang of lust he felt.

You're going to be spending a lot of time in that house. You might even see him once in a while. Hear his voice. Catch his eye. Tempt him just for the fun of it.

Adam's cell phone buzzed in his pocket. It was Victor. It was like he'd somehow been able to detect Adam's thoughts. *For some reason I just wanted to say hello. To let you know I was daydreaming about us. Like I always do.*

"I got the job," Adam announced to his new friend.

Myrtle Brubaker grinned as she pulled into the train station. "Well, then. I guess me and you will be spending some time together."

Adam opened the door. A train was arriving. He'd have to make a run for it if he wanted to catch it.

"Nothing would make me happier," he said.

CHAPTER FIVE

Stacey was on her third breadstick. Becca was on her second glass of red wine. Victor was unusually quiet.

Adam kept waiting for the right moment to make his announcement.

The Italian restaurant wasn't crowded for a Friday night. The dimly lit dining room was enhanced by the ambience of low-playing accordion music, flickering votive candles, and the constant aroma of garlic and butter drifting in the air.

Adam looked at Victor's profile, reminding himself of just how attractive he was. They were sitting across the table from his mother and his roommate.

It was the first time they'd been together in almost two days. Victor had texted he was working extra hours at his office temp job and putting in some effort on a new art project. Adam responded that he had a lot of homework. They were avoiding each other, and Adam wasn't sure why.

They were finished eating. Everyone at the table seemed to be slipping into a food-induced state of sleepiness.

"This place is a ghost town tonight," Adam said. "It's usually packed in here."

His mother nodded. "Everyone hears the word *blizzard*

and they hibernate. Even in Chicago. You'd think we'd be used to it by now."

Something is bothering Victor. I can tell. Does he want to be somewhere else? I need to talk to him. Alone.

"Thank you all for celebrating my new promotion," Becca said, raising her glass.

"Thank you for paying," Stacey replied with a grin. "You probably feel like you've got three kids instead of one, Becca."

Becca smiled. "Sometimes, yes. But no complaints. I'm happy my son has both of you in his life."

Adam smiled, hoping Victor would do the same. He didn't. "Don't get any ideas, Stacey," Adam said. "I enjoy being an only child. Besides, Victor and I are not brothers and we never will be."

"Why not?" Stacey teased.

"Because it would complicate…things."

Becca leaned in. "Oh?"

Adam saw the look his mother gave him. Did she know? Had she figured it out? That after three years, he and Victor were going to become more than friends?

My God, she'd do a cartwheel in the middle of the restaurant if I told her we were falling in love.

Adam looked around the table and said, "I have an announcement to make."

Victor shifted in his chair. Adam could feel Victor's eyes on him. He was surprised when he felt Victor's hand land on his thigh under the table. He could feel the heat from Victor's palm through his pants. Other than their all-too-brief makeout session two nights ago, it was the first time Victor had touched Adam in such an intimate manner.

He's claiming me. He's reminding me I'm his.

Adam swallowed. "I got the job," he said, expecting shouts of glee and high-fives.

At once, Victor pulled his hand away. Adam looked at Victor for an explanation, but his companion was avoiding his eyes. Victor sat there with disappointment on his face. He looked wounded and crushed.

Did I do something wrong? Why is he upset with me?

"That's fantastic news," Becca said. "I knew this would happen for you. When do you start?"

"Monday."

"Monday?" Stacey repeated. "We need to celebrate. What should we drink?"

"It's part-time?" Becca asked.

Adam nodded. "I think so. Mrs. Vassalo said we'd work around my school schedule."

Wait. Did she actually say that? I don't remember.

"I've been lying low and hiding out from the landlord this week," Stacey said. "So, fill me in, please. What job is this?"

"My mother hooked me up with this rich guy who hired me to tutor his daughter in English. She wants to write mysteries. Apparently, I'm supposed to teach her how."

Stacey couldn't hide her shock. "You're a teacher?"

"No. Just a tutor."

Stacey shook her head. "Someone's trusting you to tutor their child? Do they know what a borderline anarchist you are?"

"Such a big word," Adam said. "You must be sober."

"Only because no one's offered to buy me a drink yet."

"You might have better luck at another table," Adam said.

"Don't pick on me," she said. "I'm selling cowboy hats to tourists while you're socializing with the elite."

"You don't mind the commute?" Becca asked. "It's a long train ride."

"Where is it?" Stacey said "Wisconsin?"

Adam grinned. "Close enough. The family lives in Lake Bluff."

"Jesus," she said, "how'd you score this gig? Good thing they didn't call me for a reference. I would've told them the truth about you."

"Mr. Vassalo is a new client of mine," Becca explained.

Victor leaned forward. "What's he do?" he asked, an angry tone underlining his words. "Why's he so rich?"

Why are you so mad? What did I do to piss you off?

"He designs new housing developments," Becca explained. "He's worth a fortune. And by the grace of God, he's decided to make our bank his preferred lender for a new multimillion-dollar project."

"I'm confused," Victor continued. "How does Adam fit into all this? Is he collateral for a business deal?"

Ouch.

"Mr. Vassalo met Adam in my office and the two of them…hit it off. He was impressed with Adam. And why shouldn't he be?"

"Does he want a girlfriend?" Stacey asked.

"He's married," Adam explained.

"I'll settle for mistress."

"Stacey—" Becca began.

"Really, Becca," she said. "I have no shame. At least I'll admit it."

"Forget it," Adam said. "I met his wife."

"And?"

"She's gorgeous and Greek. You wouldn't stand a chance in hell."

Victor stood up. He looked at everyone at the table, except for Adam.

"I'm sorry," he said. "I'm not feeling well."

"What's wrong?" Becca asked, her eyes narrowed with concern.

Victor shook his head. "I think I need to go."

Becca reached for her purse. "Let me give you cab fare."

"I'll be fine," he said. "I'm going to walk."

"But a storm is coming," she reminded him.

"I need the air," he said.

Apparently, Becca didn't want to take *no* for an answer. "I can drive you," she offered. "I have my car. I don't want you walking through a blizzard, Victor."

"No, really. I'm fine," he said. "I promise. I'm sure I'll feel better soon. Thank you."

Although he wasn't sure why, Adam reached out to grab the sleeve of Victor's sweatshirt. Just as his fingers were about to make contact, Victor slipped away. Before he could say another word, Victor was out the front door.

He didn't even say good-bye.

Adam glanced across the table. Becca and Stacey were both staring at him with confusion.

"What is going on?" Becca asked. "Did you two have a fight?"

"Not that I'm aware of," Adam said. "I don't know what's wrong. Maybe it was something I said. He's been super sensitive lately."

"He needs to grow a pair and get over it," Stacey said.

Becca signaled to the waiter with a gentle wave. "I'm ordering a cappuccino. Anyone else?"

"I'll take a shot of tequila," Stacey said. "You know, to keep warm during the blizzard tonight."

"How about some cab fare instead?" Becca offered. "Do you mind taking a cab?"

Stacey shrugged. "Not if you're paying."

"I want to drive my son home," Becca explained. "I think we need to talk."

❖

They were parked at the end of the block, a few doors down from the apartment building where Adam and Stacey lived. Above them, a corner street lamp burned through the icy haze, hugging them with a pool of pale orange light.

Adam constantly teased his mother about her car, referring to it as the Granny Mobile. He didn't see the appeal. It was oversized and moved slow.

Becca left the motor idling and the heater on. Outside, the snow was getting heavier.

Adam knew his mother was tired. He could hear it in her voice. "I'm worried about all three of you," she said. She turned the radio down.

"Did you drive me home for some lecture time?"

"I don't lecture you."

"You don't?"

"Do I?"

"Sometimes you just can't help yourself," Adam said.

"I never thought of myself as that type of mother. I'm just being helpful."

"Mom, we're adults," Adam reminded her. "We've done fine so far."

"I know you have," she said. "Much better than I handled things at your age."

Adam glanced out the window. The sidewalk was empty. There wasn't a soul in sight. Maybe his mother's theory about hibernation was true. Maybe he needed to get inside and urge her to get home before the blizzard. "Your situation was completely different," he said. "I know that."

"Yes, but I never resented it," she said. "Not for a second."

"No?"

Becca sighed. "I just thank God for your grandfather. I don't know if I would've made it through without him."

"Me either."

"He's a good man," she said. "So is Victor."

He shot his mother a look. "Is that what this is about? And here you were doing so well, Mother."

"I see how he looks at you," she said. "Your father used to look at me the same way when we first met. In the beginning. I remember."

She sounds so sad. Be nice to her. She needs it. She's lonely. Adam softened his tone. "I'm sure you guys really loved each other," he said.

"Yeah, but we were so young," she said. "I don't know if we really understood what it all meant. We were just two kids who grew up in the same neighborhood. Sort of like you and Victor."

She's incorrigible. She's not going to give up until Victor and I are walking down the aisle.

"Mom, Victor grew up in Pilsen. We lived in Rogers Park."

"You know what I mean. You've known each other for a long time now."

"Three years."

"That's two years longer than I had with your father."

"Why so nostalgic tonight?" he asked.

"I still miss him," she said. "I know a lot of time has passed and everyone thinks I should've moved on. I mean, my God, it's been over twenty years. But…I just couldn't."

Adam took a breath and asked a question he never thought he would. "Why didn't you stop him?"

"From joining the military?" she said. Adam nodded in response. "It was his dream. How do you stop someone from something they want so badly?"

"You could've begged him to stay. You could've told him it was the wrong decision."

"But it was the right one for him."

"It wasn't," Adam said. "Otherwise, he'd be here with us. And you wouldn't be sitting outside my apartment on a Friday night in the Granny Mobile trying to convince me Victor is the perfect man for me."

"The war was your father's destiny. There's nothing any of us could've done to stop it from happening."

"His fate was to step on a land mine and be blown away?"

"I didn't say it made sense to me," she said. "How he died. He was always so careful. He knew he was coming home in two weeks. He knew I was pregnant with you. Your grandfather had already lined up a job for him. Everything was going to be perfect again."

"Maybe he made a mistake," Adam said. "People do make mistakes, Mom."

"I certainly know I have," she said. "Have you?"

"Yes," he said. "For one, I know I shouldn't have waited so long…with Victor."

Her smile lit up the car. "I was right?"

"Don't sit there and look like you just won the lottery."

She was beaming. "I knew it. I told you. The two of you belong together."

"Okay. I'll admit it. You were right."

"Anyone who spends more than five minutes with the two of you can tell."

"Well, I finally came to my senses," Adam said.

"And how does Victor feel?"

"Not as ecstatic as you, but close."

"You have no idea how happy this makes me."

"What has that promotion done to you?"

"It's worn me out, Adam. This has been one of the longest weeks of my life. I'm so worried...I don't wanna screw this up."

"You're good at what you do," he said. "Everyone at the bank knows that."

"I don't know," she said. "We foreclosed on a family. The husband keeps calling me. He cries on the phone and begs me to help him. I'm worried he's going to do something foolish because he's so distraught. He's lost everything."

"It happens to a lot of people," Adam said. "It's very sad. He's one of many."

"But he's the first for me. How do I tell someone I can't help them? My loyalty is to the bank. He doesn't want to hear that. What do I say to him? 'Joe, I'm sorry you and your family will be sleeping in your car in the dead of winter in Chicago and no government program in the entire state of Illinois will help you, but things will get better. Just keep your chin up, my friend.'"

"You can't save the world, Mom."

"I wish I could," she said. "Honestly, I'd give anything to save the people we've lost."

"Dad?"

"Your dad," she said. "Victor's little brother."

"Victor hasn't really mentioned him since the funeral last year."

"I still think about him all the time," she said. "I was there. Remember? Just be glad you weren't. You didn't see what happened to him. It was awful. He died right there on the sidewalk in front of the bank. In broad daylight. It still scares me."

"All of these people…they're from our past, Mom. This is now."

"I was so afraid you were going to be all alone," she said.

"Me?"

"You can't be Stacey's roommate for the rest of your life, Adam."

"She needs someone to hold her hair back when she pukes."

"Are you and Victor going to move in together?"

She's lost her mind.

"No," Adam said. "I think we're running away together to Paris."

"Be serious."

"I am," he said. "Sort of. There's a private art school there that he really wants to go to. So he can become a famous sculptor. He's so incredibly talented."

"What's stopping him?" she asked.

"He applied back in November. They haven't made their decision yet. If he gets in, I think he'll wait for me to graduate in June so we can go to Paris together. He'll go to school and make beautiful art. Maybe I'll get a decent job and write some clever words for an ad agency. Life will be amazing then. The only problem is we studied German and Victor speaks Spanish, so we'll have to learn French."

"How'd you get so lucky?" she said. "Victor is a wonderful man."

"Maybe he's *my* destiny," Adam said.

"Now you're making fun of me."

"No, I'm not," he said. "Okay…maybe I am. But just a little."

"Are you scared?" she asked.

"About the new job?"

"No. About being with Victor. About a relationship. You've never had one before."

"Why should we be scared?"

"I was."

"Everything makes you nervous."

"Your father did," she said.

"Is that how you got pregnant? Because you were too afraid to say no?"

"In a way, yes."

"Seriously?"

"Once he told me he enlisted, I was worried he was going to go away and never come back."

"It's sad to say, but it looks like you were right," Adam said.

"I wanted to have a piece of him forever." She turned and looked at Adam. "And I do."

"Lucky you."

"You look so much like him, Adam. He was tall and skinny just like you. You have the same hands. The same smile. But completely different personalities."

This conversation is getting way too serious for me. I wonder what Stacey's doing upstairs. I think I need a drink. I know she's got some tequila stashed in the back of the freezer.

"I've been working out," he said, hoping the subject would change.

"Have you?"

"I don't think it shows yet."

"You're handsome just the way you are. I'm sure Victor agrees with me."

"I don't know what happened to him at the restaurant. We haven't really talked or hung out for a couple of days."

"Maybe he's got a lot on his mind."

"Maybe," he said. "Or maybe he and I just got a little freaked out."

The voice coming from the car radio caught Becca's attention. "I haven't heard this song in ages," she said. "For so long, I couldn't listen to it."

"Why? Who is this?"

"Cyndi Lauper," she said.

"Don't know her."

"You're too young. It's one of my favorites. I love the whole album."

"I've never heard it before."

"It's called 'Money Changes Everything.'"

"That's weird," Adam said.

She looked hurt. "You don't like it? It's a really special song to me."

"Actually, I do. It's just…that phrase…this is like the third time I've heard those words this week. You don't think that's strange?"

"Maybe the universe is trying to tell you something."

"What, that I'm broke? I don't need a song or a poster to remind me of that. I can go online and look at my bank account and see the truth."

"Do you need some cash?" she asked. "Until you get your first paycheck?"

Oh, shit. I have no idea how much the Vassalos are going to pay me. I forgot to ask.

"No," he said. "I'll manage. I always do."

Becca caressed the top of the steering wheel with two fingertips. "It was playing on the radio when I got home that night," she explained. She lifted her eyes and stared through the windshield. Adam wondered if she could see the memory.

"This song?" he asked.

She nodded. "I was seven months pregnant at the time. I was working as many shifts as I could at Dominick's."

"The grocery store? I never knew you worked there. I only remember you at the bank."

"The days were very long. I was constantly on my feet there. It was taking a toll on me, but I had rent to pay. And your grandmother still hadn't forgiven me for ruining her son's life. I had no one back then."

"The military didn't help you?" Adam asked.

She nodded. "Thank God we got married right before he was deployed," she said. "Best decision we ever made. It was his idea. He said it was something we had to do. Just in case something went wrong. But I wasn't making much, even with what the government was giving me and what I was making at the store."

"Sounds like a really tough time," he said. "Honestly, I don't know how you got through it."

"I remember driving home that night," she continued. Adam could see a faint reflection of the street lamp in her eyes. "It was snowing. Not as much as it is right now. One of the windshield wipers on the car wasn't working right, so it was hard to see. I was nervous driving home. I kept thinking, *Just a few more weeks. Just a few more weeks and he'll be home. Everything will be all right then.*"

Adam was afraid to ask. He'd only heard bits and pieces of the story before. Never had Becca been so forthright with the details. "What happened?"

Adam watched as his mother tilted her head back against her seat and closed her eyes. "This song was on the radio," she said. "I was singing along with it to try to take my mind off everything. I kept focusing on what she was singing about. The words made so much sense to me in that moment."

"Yeah," Adam said. "They do to me, too."

"I pulled into the driveway. The house was really little. Just one bedroom and a little yard with a patch of dead grass out front. Not much to look at. But it was ours for the time being. When I got there, there were two men standing on the front porch. They were in uniform. They were waiting for me. Before I even got out of the car, I knew."

❖

Adam found him sitting in the stairwell, not far from the front door of his apartment. Their eyes met. Even in the dull light of the bare bulb burning above them, Adam could tell Victor had been crying.

"Victor, what are you doing here?" he asked. "I thought you went home."

Victor looked into Adam's eyes as if he were searching for something. "You don't look happy to see me," he said. His voice sounded defeated.

"I am. Of course, I am. I'm just…surprised."

Victor lowered his eyes. "You've hardly said two words to me since you got that job."

Is that true? Have I been ignoring him? Wait. I thought

he needed some space. I thought he was off working extra hours and sculpting.

"You said you were working a lot of hours this week. I didn't want to bug you."

"I don't understand what's going on," Victor said. "Between us."

Adam sat down next to him. They were squeezed together between the cracked wall and the marred wooden banister. "Me either," Adam said. "Everything feels weird now. And we haven't even done anything."

"Is it me?" he asked. "Did I change overnight? Because I still feel like the same Victor I've been for the last three years. I'm still here...waiting for you to make a move, to tell me you feel the same way."

"I thought I already did. The other night. Here."

"You sent me away," he said. "With some lame-ass thing about me being too good for you."

"We both know you are."

Victor's voice rose. "No. We both know that's bullshit."

"Can you not yell, please? I don't need all of my neighbors to know our business."

"Are you ashamed of me, is that it?"

"Victor, have you lost your mind?"

"Answer the question."

"No, I'm not ashamed of you."

"Not even just a little bit?" he asked. "Maybe I'm not the type of guy you see yourself with. Maybe because I don't have a perfect body or because I'm not rich. Maybe you're having second thoughts because the truth is it's *you* who's too good for *me*."

Adam was worried he might start to cry again.

This is all my fault. I can't believe I've made him feel this way. I'm so dumb. I was just working this out in my head. Victor, I'm sorry. I need to tell you so…

Adam slipped his arm through Victor's. He lowered his voice to a calm whisper, hoping it had an effect. "Can we go inside please?" he said. "I'll make us some coffee. We can talk. For as long as you want."

"That's not an option. Stacey's home. She's… entertaining."

"Who's she with?"

"She didn't say. I knocked. She texted me and said go away."

Don't give up. Don't let the night end like this.

Adam stood up. He moved toward the door of his apartment. He fished the key out of the front pocket of his jeans. "We can go to your place, then," he said. "Let me get some clothes. I'll spend the night. We can spend the entire weekend together. It's snowing. It'll be perfect. Romantic, even."

Behind him, he heard Victor speak. "I got in."

The moment felt suspended in the space between them.

"What?" Adam said, already knowing but not wanting to hear the words.

"To the art school," Victor said. "In Paris. I got the letter today."

Adam took a breath before he spoke. "Why didn't you tell me?"

Victor stood. They were face-to-face. He reached for both of Adam's hands and held them in his own. "Because I haven't decided if I'm going to accept their offer."

"My God, why wouldn't you?"

"I have until the first of March to decide."

"What's there to even consider, Victor?" he said. "You've been talking about that school for almost two years. Of course you're going."

Victor tightened his grip on Adam's hands. "Only if you're going with me."

"How can I do that?"

"You get a passport. You pack a bag. You get on the plane."

"You know it's not as simple as that," Adam said. "I'm not finished with school. The semester isn't even half over."

"I don't start school there until summer."

"Then what's the issue? You e-mail them back and tell them yes."

"Only if you make me a promise. Right here, right now."

"In the stairwell? It smells like cat piss out here. I hate this building."

"Don't ruin the moment."

"I'm not trying to. Honest."

"Promise me you'll go with me to Paris," Victor said. "And then we can do whatever you want for the rest of the weekend. For the rest of our lives."

Adam pulled his hands away. "There's a lot to think about."

The hope dimmed in Victor's eyes. The hurt returned. "I understand."

"You look angry again."

"I'm not," Victor said.

"Now you're lying to me."

"I've never lied to you."

"Well, don't start tonight," said Adam.

"Do you regret it?" Victor asked. "Telling me you wanted to take things further between us?"

"No. Of course not. I meant it."

"Are you sure?"

"Everything just feels so…different," Adam said. "Just a couple of days ago we were laughing and having fun. How did it all get so serious so fast? I feel like something bad happened. Like someone died."

"Then what do we do, Adam?"

"I don't know."

"It's not supposed to be like this," he said. "You and I both know we're supposed to be together."

"Yes."

"If that's the case, then why are we fucking this up so bad?" Victor said.

Adam slid into Victor's arms. They closed their eyes in unison and held on.

"Help me fix it," Adam said. "Help me make it right."

Adam tried to pull away but Victor didn't want to let go. "I love you so much that I give you permission."

"Permission?" Adam repeated. "To do what?"

"Whatever it is you have to do to figure out if it's me you want to be with."

"I already know I do," Adam said. "I have from the beginning. Since we met."

"Then I'll be waiting," said Victor. "Until the first of March."

"For what?"

"For you," he said. "For your heart."

CHAPTER SIX

She was sitting at the piano with her arms folded across her chest, with what looked like a permanent pout on her face. Adam watched her for a moment from where he stood in the open doorway of the formal living room, worried she would hate him.

His eyes moved to the massive floor-to-ceiling window. The thick green drapes were opened. The afternoon sky was overcast. Gray-white light streamed in through the window, covering her young face with a hazy glow. Her eyes were lowered. She was staring at the piano keys so intently, Adam wondered if she were trying to force them to play by using some form of mind control.

She's crazy. She looks it. I can tell already. Shit. She saw me.

Anastasia sensed Adam's presence. She turned her neck so fast, Adam feared the child had given herself whiplash.

Their eyes locked.

Her hair was dark and long, like her mother's. It was pulled back into a messy ponytail. Her eyes were a cool blue. Her stare was so intense, he was certain she could see right through him.

She was wearing a navy blue and white school uniform,

but the look didn't suit her. She crossed her feet at the ankle and said, "Whatever my parents said about me…it's not true. I'm actually a lot worse than they think I am."

Her sweet voice didn't match the tough, know-it-all persona she was desperately trying to portray. Beneath the moody, scowl-like expression was a twelve-year-old girl who had a big heart.

Adam grinned and approached. "Actually, they didn't tell me anything about you," he lied. "Except for the fact you want to write novels. Mysteries, I believe. I assume you like to tell stories about ghosts and haunted houses? Or detectives trying to solve a case?"

"I want to write about murder, "she said. "I like Edgar Allan Poe."

Adam gave a slight shrug. "Who doesn't?"

Anastasia stood up. "Look at me," she said. "Do you think I'm a dork?"

He almost laughed.

Poor thing. To be a kid again.

"I don't really know you," he said. "Why should my opinion even matter?"

"You didn't answer my question," she said. "I'm waiting."

"You seem cool to me," he said.

She lit up like a Christmas tree. "I do?" she said. "The kids at school think I'm a dork. Just because I like to read and hang out in the library."

Adam smiled and said, "You're too pretty to be a dork."

She was elated, but the dark cloud returned. "I'm not as pretty as my mother."

Adam shook his head and said, "Nobody is."

"She's not as perfect as you think," Anastasia replied.

"I could tell you things about her. But I could tell you even more about him. It might shock you."

"How old are you?" he asked.

She moved to the window. She turned her back to him. She looked out at the circular driveway and the huge stone water fountain. There was a marble cherub statue in the center of it. "Old enough to know I'll never be as pretty as my mother," she said. "I'm twelve."

Adam sat down at the piano. "Seventh grade?"

She shook her head. "Eighth. I skipped a year."

"Which one?"

She looked at him. "Does it matter?"

"Probably not."

"I skipped the second grade. I'd like to skip the rest of them and go straight to college."

She's smarter than half the people I know. Maybe more.

"Northwestern?" he asked.

She rolled her eyes. "Oxford."

"Must be nice."

She moved close to him. She leaned over the rounded edge of the piano to get a better look. She was inspecting him. "You don't look like a teacher," she decided. "You're too young."

"What do I look like?"

"Like a boy who works at a bookstore. Or some place with a lot of plants. A nursery. You look like you should be watering really pretty flowers. Do you do that on the side?"

"I'm not a teacher," he said. "And I don't work at a bookstore and I've killed every plant I've ever owned. I'm in school."

Anastasia looked confused. "For what?"

"For punishment," he said. This made her giggle. "That's what it feels like. I'm almost done. I graduate in June."

"Oh." She sat down beside him on the shiny black piano bench. "Then what will you do?"

Good question. You should be a guidance counselor, kid. Or join forces with my mother. She would adore you.

"I'm thinking about Paris," he said. "At least for a year or two."

"I've been there twice," she said. "It's dirty. The people are rude."

"Sounds like my kind of town."

"So, what are we doing?"

"What do you mean?" he asked.

"Aren't you here to turn me into some sort of literary genius? Didn't they hire you to help me write a future bestseller? Or are you just a babysitter?"

"Not sure I can promise those kinds of results. And it seems like you've got the genius part down."

"I already like you better than the other ones."

"I'm not your first tutor?"

"God, no," she said. "All the tutors my father finds for me are men. *Young* men. They're all good-looking. Maybe he's hoping I'll fall in love with one of them and then he'll be rid of me once and for all. I'm just in the way around here."

"You're twelve and you're already thinking about marriage? Maybe I'm supposed to talk some sense into you."

"My parents think I'm difficult," she said with pride. "I'm sure they warned you."

She likes the title. Don't give it to her. Make her earn it.

"No," he said. "Not really."

"They didn't tell you about my behavioral problems at school?"

"What did you do?"

"I punched a girl in the mouth and busted her lip open wide. She bled everywhere and told the principal I threatened to kill her in her sleep."

"Did you do it?" he asked.

"Those weren't my exact words to her…so…no."

"Your parents never mentioned it," he said. "Maybe they think you've changed."

She was on her feet again. "I think they're assholes."

"That sounds harsh."

"She's always angry. He's always gone. She's lonely. He's arrogant. I got stuck living with them against my will," she said. She was back at the window. She placed both palms flat against the glass and said, "I've been planning my escape since I was four."

"Then what will you do, Anastasia?"

"Leave," she said. "And never look back."

❖

Adam knew the hour was late without even glancing at the chiming grandfather clock in the foyer. With his charcoal gray pea coat draped over his arm, he stood in the doorway of what looked to be a home library. The room was located directly on the opposite side of the foyer from the formal living room, where he'd spent most of the afternoon and part of the evening with Anastasia.

Dario was sitting next to the fire, engrossed in a pile of documents in his lap. Adam remained silent and unnoticed, watching and admiring Dario. The older man was wearing a pair of reading glasses. They only made him look sexier. He was dressed for bed in a silk robe, silk pajama bottoms, black slippers.

All he needs is a pipe.

Adam could see it was snowing outside through a large bay window.

Dario sensed Adam's presence. He turned to the doorway. His mouth curled up into a smile. He stood, placing his pile of papers on the love seat he'd just occupied. As he moved, his robe came untied at the waist and opened.

"Join me," he said.

Adam lowered his eyes, desperately trying not to look at Dario's chest. He moved to where Dario stood in front of the fireplace. The flames cast an orange glow over their skin.

"I hope I'm not bothering you," Adam said to his boss. "I know it's late. I think I lost track of time. If it weren't for Jane, Anastasia and I probably would've worked until midnight."

"I'm reading financial reports," Dario said. "You're a wonderful distraction. I should be thanking you."

Adam raised his eyes, allowing himself just one quick peak at Dario's dark chest hair, his half-erect nipples, the taut abs.

Damn. Why does he have to be so attractive? I bet he's a great kisser.

"I'm done for the day," he said. "Tutoring your daughter. She gave me a personal tour of your beautiful house. All you need is a dungeon."

"I had a wine cellar built a few years ago, but no dungeon, I'm afraid." Dario took a step closer. "I hope Ana isn't giving you too much trouble," he said. "She can be difficult at times."

"So I've been told," said Adam. "But I don't find her difficult at all."

Dario grinned. "Well, that's a first. You must be good at what you do."

Adam took a deep breath, unable to look away from Dario Vassalo—the thick, dark hair. The smoldering dark eyes. The chiseled jaw. The permanent five o'clock shadow. The perfect teeth. The sweet smell of his olive skin.

This man is the epitome of sexy.

"In fact," he said, trying to stay focused on what he was saying, "Anastasia and I get along great."

"Excellent," Dario said. He placed a palm on Adam's back and patted him a few times. "I hope in due time you can say the same about me."

Adam glanced down quickly. He licked his lips and tried to ignore the heat the fire was throwing off. He could clearly make out the outline of Dario's cock through the silky fabric of his pajama bottoms.

Don't look at him. Think of something else. He'll catch you staring at his cock.

Adam looked up and met Dario's stare. He could see the reflection of the fire, flickering in Dario's dark eyes. "I've never gotten the chance to thank you," he said.

"Thank me?" Dario said. "For what?"

"For the job. For this opportunity," he said. "I'm very happy to be here."

Dario glanced down at the bulge in his pajamas. "Obviously I'm happy as well," he said with a gentle laugh. He placed a hand over his crotch. "You have to forgive me. I'm a little embarrassed here. Clearly, it has a mind of its own."

"It's okay," Adam said. "It happens."

Dario opened his robe a little wider. "It's warm."

"It's the fire," Adam said.

Dario raised an eyebrow. "Is it?"

Adam felt uncomfortable, awkward, and incredibly aroused. He shifted the coat he was holding to the opposite arm. "Should we call Myrtle to come pick me up now?"

Dario didn't hide his disappointment. "I'll take care of it for you," he said. "I suppose you want to get home."

Do I have another choice? If I stay here much longer we'll be naked within seconds, having hot sex in front of the fire.

Dario reached into a pocket in his robe for his cell phone and sent a text. "She should be here in a few moments," he said.

Adam turned away from the heat and moved toward the doorway. "I can wait outside. I'm sure you have work to do."

Besides, your wife made it very clear I was to stay out of your way and leave you alone.

"It can wait," he said. "Sit with me."

Adam sat on a cream-colored love seat positioned in front of a potted palm.

He glanced over at Dario, who pushed his pile of paperwork aside. A few sheets floated down to the carpet.

I wish I was sitting in your lap, Mr. Vassalo.

"I want you to feel welcome here," Dario said.

"Thank you. I do."

"If you need anything—anything at all—just ask Jane."

"Does she live here with you?" Adam asked.

"Yes. She's been with us since we lived in Greece. We brought her here with us. She's part of our family."

I want to crawl across this floor to you, slide between

your legs, pull those pajama bottoms down and take your cock into my mouth.

Dario opened his legs a little wider, offering a perfect view of the outline of his half-hard cock pressing against his silky pants. "I'm worried," he said. "It's late. Will you be all right taking the train home?"

Adam grinned. "I guess I'm a lot like Anastasia," he said, only half-joking. "I'm tougher than I look."

Dario was intrigued. "Really?"

"I've been working out lately."

He raised an eyebrow. "Have you?"

"Yes."

Dario leaned forward in his chair. "Show me," he said.

Adam felt his cheeks pale. Nervousness coated his tongue. "What?"

"Let's see."

Adam waited to see if Dario was serious. Finally, he stood up. "Okay," he said.

"Come here," Dario said. "Closer."

Adam obeyed. He moved across the room. He stood over Dario and stared down at him. He lifted his arm and flexed a muscle.

Two can play at this game, Dario.

"Feel," Adam said.

Dario reached up and slipped a hand around Adam's bicep. "Nice," he said. "And what about the rest of you?"

Fear tickled the roof of Adam's mouth. "What do you mean?" he asked, hoping his nerves didn't show.

"Lift your shirt," Dario said.

Adam hesitated for a moment. No one had ever looked at his body before. He felt very self-conscious. He thought about refusing, but he couldn't. He lifted his shirt, revealing his smooth, pale skin. Dario slid two fingers across Adam's abs and up to his chest. He pinched one of Adam's pink nipples. He shuddered.

"Even better," Dario said. "It seems you're right, Adam. You're tougher than you look."

Adam felt his own cock hardening. He lowered his shirt and turned away. "I can take care of myself," he said.

"I imagine you've been doing that for most of your life."

"My mother and my grandfather helped me," he said. "They still do when they can."

Dario was on his feet again. Adam could feel the man standing behind him, his breath covering the skin on the back of Adam's neck.

"Everybody needs somebody, right?"

Adam turned and faced his boss. "Who do *you* need?" he asked.

"Someone who understands me. Someone who can anticipate what I want," he said. "I think you understand me, Adam."

"I think we understand each other," he agreed. He lowered his voice to a whisper. "But I don't think your wife would understand this at all."

"This isn't about her."

"Isn't it?" Adam said, glancing at the open doorway, expecting Jane or Evangelina to be there, watching them. "In case you haven't noticed, this is her house, too."

The muscles in Dario's jaw tightened. There was an edge to his tone of voice now. "She and I have…an arrangement."

Yeah, I bet you do.

"I'm intrigued. Enlighten me."

"I do what I want. She pretends not to notice."

"How convenient for you," Adam said.

"It's a complicated situation."

"Being a married man who prefers the company of other men?" Adam said. "Yes, I have to agree. That *is* very complex. Why not just be single and do whatever you want without having to hide?"

"We were married to please our families," said Dario. "There's an agreement in place."

Adam walked away. He stopped in the doorway and looked back. "A promise is a promise," he said.

"You've never made a promise to someone you couldn't keep?"

The only promise I intend on keeping is the one I made to Victor to run away to Paris with him. Because we're in love. Something you clearly know nothing about, Dario Vassalo.

"I'm not perfect," Adam said. "I'll be the first to admit that."

Dario's eyes drifted over Adam's body, from head to toe. "What if I think you are?" he said.

Adam shook his head. He slipped on his coat and buttoned it. "I'm sorry," he said. "I'm not interested."

"What *would* you like, Adam? Are you not interested in what I'm offering to you?"

Outside, the cab arrived. The headlights washed across the bay window, illuminating the home library, the truth of the matter.

Myrtle Brubaker to the rescue.

"I would like to go home," Adam decided. He started to walk away.

Dario followed. His words stopped him. "You're forgetting something."

Adam kept his eyes on the front doors. "And what's that?"

Don't turn around. Don't look at him.

Dario stood behind Adam. He reached around him and held up his hand. Between his fingers were a few hundred dollar bills. "This should cover your fair share of the rent," he whispered into Adam's ear.

Adam stepped away "I can't take that. It's too much money. I only worked for a few hours today."

Dario moved fast. He grabbed the boy, turned him around, and shoved him against the front door.

"You're crazy," Adam breathed.

Their mouths were close enough to kiss.

Dario reached down and slid the money into the front pocket of Adam's jeans. His fingertips brushed over the tip of Adam's hard cock. Adam let out a soft moan. "You'll soon find out I never take no for an answer," Dario said. "Remember that."

❖

"You all right? You look a little flushed."

"I'm fine, Myrtle," Adam said from the backseat of the cab. "Thank you for asking."

"You sure? Because you don't look the same as you did when I dropped you off this afternoon."

"Maybe it's the weather."

Myrtle searched for Adam's eyes in the rearview mirror. "He try something on you?" she asked. "You can tell me if he did. I got so many secrets to take to my grave, they're gonna need an extra casket."

"You know, don't you?" Adam said. "About their arrangement? The Vassalos' marriage."

"I don't know nothing about an arrangement, but I see enough to figure things out. I'm no fool. I got my suspicions."

Of course Myrtle would know everything. She's the driver. How many other male tutors have been dropped off in her shiny yellow cab?

"I'm not the first young man to be driven to this house, am I?" Adam asked.

Myrtle shook her head. "You're not the first, no. And by the look on your face, I'd say ya ain't gonna be the last."

"There's been many?" It was a statement rather than a question.

Myrtle nodded and made a left turn. "Yes."

"How many?"

"I'm a lady who keeps her mouth shut, Adam. If Mr. Vassalo wants you to know that information, he'll tell you."

"Fine," he said. "I hope they pay you well for your services."

"Want my advice?"

"Please. I need some."

"Don't go gettin' all mixed up in sumpin' you can't handle. You seem like a good kid."

"I am, for the most part."

"Then remember what you're here for."

The money felt like it was on fire in Adam's pocket. "It's just a job," he said.

Myrtle pulled into the train station. "Exactly."

❖

The train was deserted. Adam sat alone beside a window. He unbuttoned his coat and closed his eyes all the way to the city, trying desperately to ignore the tantalizing images stalking his mind.

He kept picturing Dario Vassalo sitting in front of the fire with the hot flames reflecting in his eyes, that penetrating look of lust in his gaze. His body. His skin. The inviting outline of his hard cock pressing against the silky pajamas, begging to be touched.

Adam shifted his thoughts to Victor.

I need to call him. I need to tell him I will go to Paris with him.

I want to spend forever with you. I love you, Victor Maldonado.

Adam was so deep in thought, he almost missed his stop.

As he stepped off the train, a new realization struck him, triggered by the relief the cash in his pocket would bring him. At least his share of the rent would get paid this month.

Maybe it's true. Maybe money really does change everything. Maybe Dario Vassalo wants me so bad he's willing to pay any price.

Maybe he's the not the only one who won't take no for an answer.

CHAPTER SEVEN

I wish you could come here every day."
Hearing this made Adam smile. He looked up from the three pages in his lap. This was all Anastasia had given him to read in the span of a week. Apparently, she wasn't all that eager to embark on her new literary career.

They were sitting opposite each other on matching velvet love seats in the formal living room.

Jane had popped in just moments ago with a plate of French cheese and crackers, which they'd finished quickly. Now they were sipping peppermint tea from porcelain cups.

"That's sweet of you to say, Anastasia. But I don't know how much my tutoring has helped you. It doesn't seem like you've written very much."

"But I have," she insisted. "I've written two short stories and a chapter of a novel."

"Where was I when this flurry of creativity was happening? I thought you said you only wanted to write while I was here."

"Now I wait until you leave before I do the actual work."

He suspected she was lying. "You changed your mind?"

"That way I can enjoy every second you're here."

She's good. Clearly, she's her father's daughter.

"When do I get to read this novel chapter and the other short story?"

"I'll give them to you on Friday to read over the weekend. But you can't tell my parents I wrote them."

"Why not?" he asked.

"I told them how much you're helping me. I said you were teaching me wonderful ways to become a better writer."

"And they believed you?"

"They usually do," she said. "But I told them I needed you here more."

"I can barely get here three days a week with my schedule. Don't forget I'm also in school. And I live in the city."

"Don't you have more fun here than you do at school?"

He thought about it. "Sometimes," he said. "But I also have homework."

"Bring it here with you. We can do our homework together."

"While I'm supposed to be teaching you? How is that fair to you?"

"We both know I'm a good writer."

"Agreed."

"In fact, for twelve I'd say I'm awesome."

"Okay. I'll go with that."

"More than likely," she said arrogantly, "I'll be published within the next year."

"If we tighten up your sentence structure and improve your narrative, then yes. It's a possibility."

"And when that happens, I'll give you all the credit,"

she said. "Maybe my father will give you a lot of money and then you'll come visit me all the time."

"I'm not here because of the money, Anastasia."

"Are you kidding?" she scoffed. "Everyone comes here for the money."

She really believes that. I can see it in her eyes.

"I come here because it's my job," he said. "But also because I enjoy spending time with you."

"Even though I'm only twelve?"

"You're very mature for your age."

"My grandmother in Greece says I have an old soul. She told my mother I was twelve going on fifty. I hope I have a bestseller by the time I'm sixteen. Then I can have a party and invite only the people I like."

"Just yesterday you told me you didn't like anybody," he said. "Except for me."

"Exactly."

"That won't be much of a party."

"We can get dressed up fancy. And everyone who comes will have to read something I've written."

"If that's the case, you need to get busy. You have a lot of work to do and not a lot of time. You'll be sixteen before you know it."

"And you'll be gone in June," she said. "Unless my father can figure out a way to make you stay."

❖

Later that evening, Adam stopped in the doorway of the library on his way out. Dario was standing at the window, a drink in his hand. He was dressed like he'd just walked out of an important business meeting. He'd taken the time to slip off his blazer and loosen his red silk tie.

"There's a storm headed this way," Dario said to the window.

He knew I was standing here without even looking at me. Maybe he can see my reflection in the glass.

Dario's gaze remained on whatever he was seeing on the opposite side of the window.

"Another one?" Adam said. "Every year the weather seems to get more brutal. I'll be surprised if we make it to March alive."

"May I offer you a drink, Adam?"

"No offense, but I'm not a scotch or whiskey kind of guy. I'm sure you don't have my favorite brand of cider."

Saying the words reminded Adam of the frequent nights he'd spent with Stacey in their usual booth at the Irish pub.

Wow. It seems so long ago since Stacey and I were there, even though it's only been a week or two. I haven't hung out with Stacey in days.

He already felt disconnected from everything he used to know in the short time he'd been making the commute from Chicago to Lake Bluff. The boy in that booth in the bar was becoming something from another world, another life.

And so was Victor.

Their all-too-polite and surface phone calls grew shorter with each conversation. Three days had now passed without a word between them.

Every time Adam stepped onto the train and headed north, he felt his old life slipping further and further away.

"Cider?" Dario repeated. "I don't think we do, but I could have Jane check the wine cellar for you just to be sure."

"There's no need," he said. "I'm headed home."

The authoritative tone in Dario's voice stopped him in his tracks. "It isn't safe for you to take the train tonight."

"But I have to get back to Chicago, Dario."

The older man turned away from the window. "Do you?"

"I have class in the morning. And homework."

"I'll have Myrtle drive you," he offered. "The weather should be better then."

"You'll have her drive me all the way to Lincoln Park?"

"She loves going into the city," Dario said. "It's not a good idea for you to travel in this weather. Something could happen to you. And then what would I do?"

"I appreciate the concern, but—"

Dario moved toward Adam. "I've already spoken to Jane," he said. "She's making up the guest room for you."

"Don't get me wrong," Adam said. "I love this house. And the idea of spending the night in a castle is appealing. And the train ride feels longer each time. And it's cold. And as usual I've forgotten a scarf and gloves because I'm an idiot."

"Then it's settled."

"Is it?"

"You're staying." Dario smiled, revealing perfect, bright white teeth. "You know I don't take no for an answer."

"I'm starting to learn that," said Adam. "It seems like you're a man who likes to get his way."

Dario turned away. "Always."

❖

Adam woke when he heard the bedroom door creak open. He opened his eyes, jarred from the depths of sleep. The ceiling above him was foreign and strange.

This isn't my apartment, not my bed.

He sat up, startled and disoriented.

Where in the hell am I?

His eyes darted to the slightly opened bedroom door. His heart began to race as a shot of instant terror surged through his body.

There's someone in the doorway. Now they're in the room. An intruder.

On impulse, Adam reached for his cell phone on the nightstand beside him, fumbling in the almost-dark room. He picked up the phone. It was dead.

Unsure where he was and still half-asleep, Adam was unable to speak.

Then he knew.

Dario was standing beside him, half-naked and doused in the strips of blue and silver moonlight coming through the bedroom window.

Dario placed a finger across Adam's lips.

"Don't worry," he said. "It's only me. I didn't mean to scare you."

"What are you doing in here?" Adam was too tired to be polite. He made no attempt to hide the agitation in his voice. "And why are we whispering?"

Dario brushed his lips against Adam's cheek. His words were muffled against Adam's skin. "I wanted to see you," he said. "I *had* to see you."

Adam was aroused. For some reason, this irritated him even more.

Remind him he's your boss. You work for him. This is just a job.

"Is something wrong?" he asked. "Is it Anastasia?"

For a moment, Adam wondered if Dario had started to cry. He could feel the older man's body tremble, shaking with emotion.

"There *is* something wrong," Dario said. "With me. All I do is think about you, Adam. Constantly. When you're not here I find myself counting the minutes until you arrive."

This can't be happening. Go back to bed. I'm sure your wife is wondering where you are.

Adam cleared his throat before he spoke. "Mr. Vassalo, not only are you a married man, you're also my boss. I work for you. You pay me. I'm a guest in your home."

"Let me touch you," Dario begged.

I need to quit this job. Now. Get up. Get dressed. Battle the blizzard and get your ass back to Chicago and charge your phone. Text Victor. Call him. Blow up his phone if you have to. Tell him there is no doubt in your mind or in your heart. You know what you want. You've always known.

And it's not this.

Dario slid his hand beneath the comforter. Adam felt his fingertips climbing up his thigh, sliding over his crotch. Dario squeezed the head of Adam's cock, which hardened at his touch.

A soft moan slipped out of Adam's mouth.

He's touching you. Stop him. Push him away.

"I think you should go," Adam said, covering his cock with both hands.

"I know you want me," Dario countered. "I see how you look at me."

"Doesn't everyone?" Adam said. "Is there a person in this world you've met who didn't find you attractive?"

"Then I'm correct," he said. "You *do* find me handsome. Let me get into bed with you."

Adam decided to use a different approach since *no* wasn't working. "Isn't your wife wondering where you are?"

Even the mention of Evangelina didn't seem to faze Dario. "Don't refuse me, Adam."

He reached for Adam's hand and placed it over the front of his pajamas. Adam felt Dario's thick cock throb hard beneath his palm. "Do you see what you to do me?"

Adam pulled his hand away and tucked it under the covers. "We can't do this."

Dario rubbed his cock through his pajamas. Within seconds, a spot of precum seeped through the fabric.

"Dario, stop," Adam said. To Adam's surprise, he did. "You shouldn't be in here. You know this isn't right. I don't care what sort of arrangement you have with your wife, I'm not *that* person."

Dario moved closer, almost climbing on top of Adam. He kissed the side of Adam's neck. "I want you," Dario breathed.

"I want you to leave now, Dario. I need to go to sleep."

"No. I can't leave you. I won't."

"I'm in love with someone."

Dario froze.

"What?" he said. "Who is he?"

"Victor Maldonado. We've known each other for three years."

"Is it serious?"

"Not yet, but I want it to be."

"Does he care for you, Adam?"

Adam nodded. "Very much. He loves me."

"And?"

"And I love him."

Dario stepped away from the edge of Adam's bed.

"Then so it is," he said, his voice heavy.

Adam watched as Dario moved to the bedroom door. It made a clicking sound when he opened it.

Outlined by the dim hallway light behind her, Evangelina stood on the opposite side of the door in her nightgown.

"Did you get lost, Dario?" she asked, her voice icy.

Dario's tone was harsh and angry. "Go back to bed. This doesn't concern you."

Evangelina spoke in a whisper but her words reached Adam. "Leave that poor kid alone," she said. "Don't do to him what you've done to the others."

Dario pulled the door shut behind him.

Relief washed over Adam, but he felt shell-shocked and overwhelmed.

I want to go home. This is no place for me. I don't belong here.

Victor, where are you?

CHAPTER EIGHT

Myrtle was sitting behind the steering wheel of the idling cab early the next morning.

Adam emerged from the house and trudged through the fresh blanket of snow to seek refuge in the backseat of the cab. He shivered once inside. Myrtle had the heater cranked up. Within seconds, Adam's skin felt damp with sweat. He unbuttoned his coat.

"They gotcha working nights now, too?" Myrtle asked. She cracked a sunflower seed between her teeth, spat the shell into a paper coffee cup, and pulled away from the massive house.

"I don't know if I ever want to come back here," he said.

"That bad, huh?" she said. "Is it the little demon daughter?"

Adam shook his head. "No," he replied. "She's fine. It's her father who's a handful."

"You gotta be careful," Myrtle said. "He's a powerful man, Adam."

"You make it sound like I should be scared of him, Myrtle."

"I'd like to tell you he's harmless, but I'd be lying to

ya if I did," she said. "I gotta tell ya sumpin'. Might spook you a little."

"I'm listening."

"I'm under strict orders from the boss himself," she said. "I'm not to let you out of my sight today, so to speak."

"What are you talking about?"

"Mr. Vassalo was very clear. I gotta drive you home. To Chicago."

"Okay," he said.

"Then to school."

"All right."

"And then right back here."

"Back here?" Adam repeated. Myrtle nodded. "I'm not even supposed to work today. I thought Anastasia was going to a school dance this evening."

"She is. And the missus is having a fancy dinner party tonight."

"Then what do they need me here for?"

"I don't know why. But I can tell ya Mr. Vassalo likes to keep some people as close to him as possible," she said. "I guess you can say that's part of his...charm."

"It's creepy is what is," he said. "And I'm already sick of it. That man doesn't control me. I don't need this job *that* bad."

"Best to just do what he says," Myrtle said. "Trust me."

"Whose side are you on here?" Adam asked. "I thought I took care of this last night."

"Last night is none of my business."

She thinks I'm sleeping with him.

"Myrtle, I made it very clear to Mr. Vassalo I have feelings for someone else."

"I'm sure he didn't take it very well."

"Apparently not."

"Probably why ya got a chaperone all day."

"I need to get a hold of Victor," he said. "I need to charge my phone."

"You can use mine if you'd like," she said.

Adam took the cell phone from Myrtle's outstretched hand, hoping he'd remember Victor's cell number. It took three tries but finally he figured out the right number and dialed. His call went directly to Victor's voice mail.

Damn it, Victor. I need you. I need to hear your voice.

"I don't know where you are but I need to see you. It's important."

Tell him you love him. Tell him you will go to Paris with him on the first of March. Let him know how stupid you've been. There is no doubt. You are his. Forever.

"Bye."

❖

"My God, you look worse than I feel," said Stacey. She was hunched over a bowl of soggy cereal at the kitchen table. Her face looked pale and sickly in the fluorescent glow of the overhead oven light. "Where've you been, Adam? It's been like days since I've seen you."

It feels good to be home. Why is there an empty bottle of tequila on the living room floor? Who is the hot mess sitting at the kitchen table in a glittery bikini top and stained sweatpants?

"Do you think I drink too much?" Stacey asked, a trail of cereal milk trickling down her chin.

"Why do you ask?"

"Because when I heard you paid our rent for the next three months, I decided to celebrate. I ended up sleeping with the pizza delivery guy," she said. "Do you think I have any reason to be concerned?"

"What are you talking about?"

"My love of liquor," she said. "Am I out of control? You're the only one who's ever completely honest with me."

"No…I mean the rent. I didn't pay three months of it in advance. I don't have that kind of money, Stacey."

"Well, someone does. The landlord brought me a receipt. It's on the fridge."

Adam took a few steps into the kitchen. Sure enough, there it was. Stuck beneath a tacky magnet was a handwritten receipt for three months' worth of rent.

"I know who did this," Adam said. He crumpled it up and tossed it in the direction of the overflowing white plastic trash can.

"Do me a favor and thank 'em for me," she said. "At least this time I didn't have to flash my tits to the landlord to get us a coupla more days."

"Have you seen Victor?"

"Victor paid our rent?"

"No, but have you seen him? I need to talk to him."

"No, he's been a ghost lately. Where have you been, by the way? I thought maybe you'd moved out."

"I was only gone for one night."

"Oh," she said. "Is that all?"

"This place is a mess."

"Somebody forgot to clean it."

"Well, tell *somebody* she needs to help out around here."

"Do you want to sit and have breakfast with me?"

"No, I'm late for class."

"Is there school today?" she asked. She put down her

spoon and lifted the cereal bowl to her mouth. "I thought it was Sunday."

Adam headed toward the bathroom. "I need to take a shower. I need to charge my phone."

"Shit, what day *is* it? Am I supposed to be at work right now?" Stacey tilted the bowl back and slurped down her cereal milk.

❖

There was a stretch limousine at the curb, waiting. She was standing outside his apartment building looking lost. She was wearing a fur coat Adam was certain was real. Her hands were shoved deep into the pockets. She wore huge, dark sunglasses. A thick red dotted scarf held her auburn-streaked hair out of her face. Her lipstick matched the shade of the scarf perfectly.

Adam's eyes moved to the empty parking spot next to the curb where Myrtle's cab had been idling when he'd entered the apartment building less than an hour ago.

I thought she wasn't allowed to let me out of her sight. Maybe I'm being fired. Thank God.

"I sent Myrtle on an errand for me," Evangelina explained. "She'll be back in fifteen minutes. I think you and I need to have a chat, Mr. Parsh."

She's going to tell me to stay away from her husband. She's going to threaten me. Maybe she has a gun tucked away somewhere in that big fur coat. I need to let her know things—that I only wanted the job and not to interfere with her marriage. I've always told Dario no.

"We can go somewhere," Adam suggested. "Somewhere warm. There's a coffee shop right around the corner."

"What I have to say to you won't take long," she said. "Then you can be on your way to school."

"I don't want to be late," he said. "And I already am."

And I need to find Victor. I have to.

"It seems my husband feels very generous where you're concerned. I've discovered that he's paid your rent."

Adam lowered his eyes. "Yes, he has," he admitted. "But I never asked him to."

"When my husband wants something, nothing will stand in his way," she cautioned. "He'll own you, Adam. Is that what you want?"

"No," he said, trying to control the trembling in his words. "I don't want your husband, Mrs. Vassalo."

She raised her sunglasses. "Are you sure about that?"

"I'm positive," he said. "You husband is a very attractive man. But I'm not interested. I don't care how much money he has."

"He has no soul," she said. "He sold it to Satan years ago when we still lived in Greece. He's made my life hell ever since."

Then why do you stay with him? Get out.

"He definitely seems aggressive," Adam said, "but evil?"

She lowered her sunglasses again, covering her eyes. "You have no idea," she said. "If he knew I was here talking with you..."

"I won't tell him."

"I appreciate that, Mr. Parsh," she said.

"Mrs. Vassalo, I'm not the horrible person you think I am. I'm just a guy who's trying to get through college. I only needed a job. In fact, I'm in love with someone. I told your husband this."

"It won't matter," she said. "I've seen what he's done before. There was another boy a lot like you. Last summer. He told Dario he wanted nothing more to do with him. He said he couldn't be bought."

"And neither can I," Adam insisted.

"That boy went missing, Mr. Parsh. No one has seen him since," she said. She lowered her voice to a deep whisper. "I don't have proof, but I have people looking into it. Jane is helping me."

"How?"

"She saw things," she explained. "Things I can't talk about."

"If you're trying to scare me, it's working," Adam said.

"I suppose you'll be at the house tonight. Even with the dinner party going on, he'll want you there," she said. "He will always want you there. So he can have you whenever he feels like it. But he'll get sick and tired of you. Soon you'll be there waiting for him, hoping and begging for one word. Just like the others. Maybe you'll be different. Maybe he'll decide to keep you." She leaned in close. "Maybe you won't go missing like Charlie Bower did."

Adam swallowed. "Myrtle said I have to be there tonight. She said I don't have a choice," he explained.

"Yes, you do," Evangelina said. Adam looked at her for an explanation, for help. "You can go now," she urged. "You can disappear."

Seconds later, Adam and Evangelina parted ways. She slid into the back of the waiting limousine. He headed toward the nearest train station.

Adrenaline started to surge through Adam as he stepped onto the train. The doors closed behind him. He searched for an empty seat, scanning the faces of strangers and wondering if one of them might work for Dario. Maybe he was being followed.

He peered through the smudged window as the train shuddered its way through and beneath the city.

Where am I going? Why am I so afraid? I'm acting like an idiot. Mrs. Vassalo was probably just trying to scare me.

He reached into his coat pocket for his cell phone. He tried Victor's number again. No luck. Straight to voice mail.

Why is he avoiding me?

Adam decided to skip class. He avoided the campus altogether. He was sure Dario knew his schedule, his every move.

I need to disappear, just like Mrs. Vassalo said. But where?

Adam rode the train to the end of the line, walked eight blocks with near-freezing wind punching him in the face. He sought refuge in a small neighborhood library. He found a computer in a far corner. He was still shivering when he sat down in front of the screen and typed the words "Charles Bower" into a search engine.

Sure enough, Mrs. Vassalo was telling the truth. The guy—who had similar features to Adam—had been missing since last year. There was no mention of Dario or his connection to the Vassalo family in any of the articles Adam found.

Adam's phone buzzed. He looked at the screen, hoping to see Victor's face on it.

He tried to hide the disappointment in his voice when he answered the call with, "Hello, Mother."

A few of the patrons in the library looked up.

"Hold on," he said. "Let me go outside."

Adam stepped through the automatic sliding doors. Immediately, he felt his heartbeat quicken and his breath caught in his throat.

Sitting outside the library was a familiar yellow cab. At the sight of him, Myrtle stepped out of the taxi and opened the back door, gesturing with a wave of her hand for Adam to get inside.

There's no escape.

"What is going on with you?" his mother asked in his ear. "Did something happen at the Vassalos? Did you get fired?"

"No," he answered. "Everything is fine, Mom."

"I just got a call from Dario Vassalo himself," she said. Her voice was strained with panic, weighted down with considerable worry. "It seems he's having second thoughts about moving forward. He's questioning his decision, Adam. About the bank being his preferred lender for the subdivision deal. Do you have any idea what could happen to me—my job—if he backs out now?"

"What makes you think I have anything to do with this?" he asked.

"I don't," she said. "I just needed to make sure."

"I just talked to Mrs. Vassalo earlier this morning, Mom. There's no problem."

"That's a relief. I just hope I can convince him."

"You can do it," Adam said.

I really don't have a choice now. The son of a bitch has me cornered. He knows the way to get to me is through my mother, since his money didn't work.

"I need you to go with me to the police tomorrow," Becca said.

"The police?" Adam repeated. "What for?"

"I need to file a restraining order."

Adam tightened his grip on the cell phone. "Against Dario Vassalo?"

"No," she said. "Of course not. Against that crazy customer who keeps calling me."

"You need to be careful, Mom," he said. "You need to protect yourself."

The image of Charlie Bower flashed in Adam's mind, the grainy yearbook photo used in every news article about him.

So do I. I need to confront Dario once and for all. I need to quit my job and get out while I can.

Adam slipped his phone back into his coat pocket. He moved toward the cab.

He locked eyes with Myrtle. "It didn't take you very long to find me," he said.

She straightened her visor. She waited until he was in the cab before she said, "It never does."

❖

Adam found Jane in the expansive kitchen, standing in the center of a constant moving stream of caterers and formally dressed servers. Without saying a word, the stern-faced older woman exuded authority.

"Any idea what I'm doing here?" he asked.

"You'll have to ask Mr. Vassalo why he's required you to be here this evening. I'm not in charge of you, Mr. Parsh," she answered.

"Any idea where I can find him?"

"At the moment he's probably sitting at the head of the dinner table," she said. "With his wife."

She hates me. She won't even look at me.

"You know I didn't ask for this job," he said. "I didn't

ask to come here tonight. I wasn't even invited to their stupid dinner party."

"That's a shame," she said. "Because you look terribly hungry for something."

Adam lowered his voice to a whisper. "I know what you think of me."

"How could you possibly?"

"I'm not like the others."

"That remains to be determined," she said. "Surely there are other more suitable positions for you elsewhere. More dignified ways to make a living."

"You think I should quit," he said.

"That's for you to decide, Mr. Parsh. Mrs. Vassalo has been very good to me," she said. Finally, she made eye contact with Adam. "Who's been good to you? Where does your loyalty lie?"

Adam took a breath. "Not here."

"Very well, then," she said. "It seems I've helped answer your question. We both know what you're doing here and who brought you."

Adam straightened his posture and said, "I'm leaving."

"Shall I call Mrs. Brubaker to come fetch you?"

"Don't bother," he said. "She's still outside waiting. I asked her not to leave without me."

Jane started to walk away.

"Tell me about Charlie Bower."

He could see her body tense. She turned back but avoided his eyes. "I have no idea," she said, loud enough for those around them to hear. But she took a step in closer so only Adam could hear her words. "Take my advice, Mr. Parsh. Never mention that name again in this house. If I were you, I'd get out as quickly as I could."

❖

Something caught Adam's attention on his way to the front door. He'd come down a different hallway, veering from his usual path to avoid being seen by the dinner guests. It was a rose-colored wooden door with a gleaming brass knob. Out of curiosity, he opened it and peered inside. Darkness greeted him. He searched on the wall for a light switch with a fumbling hand.

Click.

Narrow wooden stairs leading down to a basement of some sorts.

The wine cellar. I found it. I'll grab a bottle and take it home with me. I'll share it with Victor to celebrate my freedom from the insanity of Dario Vassalo. We can make a toast to our new life together in Paris.

Adam reached the bottom of the stairs. The cavernous, refrigerated room was filled with endless shelves and rows of wine bottles.

He reached for one on impulse.

The deep voice came from behind him. "Looking for something?"

Standing at the top of the stairs was Dario, in a tuxedo.

Adam stepped away from the untouched wine bottle. He moved closer to the stairs. Dario was blocking the doorway with his body.

I've been caught. And there's no way out. Fuck.

"I was just curious," Adam offered. "I wanted to know what's down here. I've never been in a wine cellar before."

Dario took a step and pulled the door shut behind him.

Adam quickly buttoned his gray pea coat as the chill in the room intensified.

This is not the place I want to be when I tell him I'm quitting my job and leaving. I need to get up those stairs. I need to get out of here.

Dario reached the bottom step. "I had it built five years ago," he said. "It was for my wife. She likes wine. A lot."

"It looks expensive," Adam said.

Dario slid his hands into the front pockets of his perfectly pleated slacks. "Appeasing my wife usually is."

Adam forced a smile. He hoped his nervousness didn't show. "What are you doing down here, Dario? Isn't there a dinner party upstairs?"

"There is," Dario said. "But they're all the same. Incredibly mind-numbing, if you want to know the truth. I make witty remarks. They laugh. I pretend to be interested in their lives. They do the same in return."

"What's the occasion?"

"The usual," he said. "I landed another new client."

"Is he here?"

"*She* is."

"What does she do?"

"She owns a large amount of land just outside Chicago," Dario said. "She's hired my firm to design a new housing tract for her. And your mother's bank will be our preferred lender. This should help prove she deserved her recent promotion, don't you think?"

Keep him talking. Soon enough he'll get bored and leave. Then you can make a mad dash for Myrtle Brubaker's cab parked outside. You'll be to the train station in less than five minutes. Then home it is. And a new life with Victor. For good.

"A subdivision?" Adam asked. "Is that what you're building?"

"An upscale one, yes," Dario said. "Luxury living."

"I wouldn't know anything about luxury living. I don't live in your world, remember?"

Dario moved closer. He slid an arm around Adam's waist. "What *do* you know about, Adam? With that hot mouth of yours, I bet you know a thing or two about sucking cock."

Don't let him know you're afraid.

"I know I should probably go back upstairs and go check on Anastasia. I saw her come in right before I came down here. She might need something. And I want to find out if she had a good time at the dance. Maybe she can write a story about it."

"She can take care of herself. She's used to it," Dario said. "Now, take off your clothes."

"She's waiting for me," Adam lied. "I promised I'd bring her a snack. I was looking for Jane. I got lost. Somehow I ended up down here."

"Lucky for the both of us you did." He licked his lips.

"Why are you looking at me like that?" Adam asked. "Don't, Dario."

"Why? You don't like it?"

"I have someone. You know that. I told you."

Dario kissed Adam's neck, brushing his soft lips across his skin. "Does it turn you on knowing when I'm looking at you I'm thinking about what I want to do to you?"

Adam took a step back. The back of his head and spine made contact with something.

Shit. It's a brick wall. I'm stuck. I need to get out of here.

"That depends," he said. "What are you thinking about?"

"What it's going to feel like to fuck you as hard as I can."

For a brief second, he imagined the sensation of feeling Dario's cock sliding in and out of his body. What it would feel like to have such a powerful man thrusting against him.

"Dario, stop touching me," he said, hoping he didn't sound frightened. "Not here. Not now."

Dario reached down between Adam's legs and squeezed his cock. "I could eat you alive," he said. "Would you like me to?"

Adam pushed Dario's hand away. "What if we get caught? Someone might wonder where you are. Why you've been gone for so long."

Dario unbuckled his belt. "I locked the door."

Of course you did.

"People might ask questions," Adam said. "Like what in the hell I'm doing here when I wasn't even invited to the party."

Dario smirked. "There's an answer for everything," he said. "You should know that by now."

Adam pushed Dario away. "I have to go," he said, moving toward the stairs.

Dario was fast. He grabbed Adam by the arm and pulled him back. Adam winced in pain. "Not so fast." Dario undid his black pants and let them slide down his legs.

I have no one to blame except myself. I'm the one who accepted the job. I knew he wanted me. I could tell from the second we met in my mother's office.

"We can't do this," Adam said. "We both know it's wrong."

"That's not true," Dario said. "You want this to happen just as much I do."

He slipped two fingers between his skin and the waistband of his red briefs. He started to lower them, maneuvering the fabric over his hard cock.

Don't do it. Don't give in. You don't love this man.

"Well, it can't happen," Adam said. "And it won't. Not ever."

"Don't say that." Dario pushed his underwear down to his knees, revealing his thick, hard cock.

Adam couldn't help it. He glanced down. The tip of Dario's cock was glistening with precum. He resisted the stirring heat between his legs, the hardening of his own cock, the temptation to pull his pants down, bend over, and let Dario pound him until he begged for mercy.

Dario wrapped a hand around his cock and started to stroke it. "I could come just looking at you," he breathed.

Adam raised his eyes. "That's not love," he said. "None of this is."

"You're so young," Dario said. "What do you know about love?"

Apparently more than you do.

"I know about the others."

Dario's eyes darkened. "What are you talking about?"

"Your appetite for younger men," Adam said. "I'm not Anastasia's first tutor. And I'm sure I won't be the last."

"You're different, Adam."

"Is that what you tell all the boys you hire? Do you drag them all down here to the wine cellar so you can have your way with them?"

"You're not in it for the money," Dario said.

"If I were, that would make me something far worse than you."

Dario grabbed Adam by the shoulders. He pushed him against a wooden beam, not far from the bottom of the narrow staircase. "You think I'm guilty of something?"

Dario pressed his half-naked body against Adam, rubbing his cock against his jeans.

Adam avoided Dario's eyes, shifting his gaze to the brick wall. It only took a second or two for Adam to notice something was different about the bottom half of the wall. The pattern of bricks didn't match the others. The variation was slight but it was there.

Adam turned his head and looked at another wall, comparing. He looked back again at the section that had caught his attention. There was definitely a difference. It was as if that section had been altered somehow, changed.

But why?

Maybe the builder had made a mistake.

Or maybe someone had replaced the original bricks with new ones because they'd placed something behind the bricks.

Or because they'd buried someone behind the wall.

Someone like Charlie Bower.

"Aren't you?" Adam said. "Do I have to keep reminding you about your wife? How can you do this to her?"

"She doesn't care. She never has."

"I'm not so sure about that. I see how she looks at me. She wishes I would go away and never come back. And that's *exactly* what I'm going to do."

Dario froze. The muscles in his jaw twitched. He spoke almost through clenched teeth. "Don't do that to me," he cautioned.

Holy fuck. He's insane. I see it. It's in his eyes. I've just set this maniac off.

Adam could hear his own voice waiver. "Dario, I graduate in June."

"Then I'll get you a job. Anything you want. Name it."

"I don't want you to do that," he said. "And I don't want you to pay my rent anymore. And stop telling Myrtle to follow me everywhere. Please get dressed."

Dario gestured down. "You don't want this?"

"I already told you…this isn't love."

"Speak for yourself."

"You can't say that. You hardly know me."

"I know I want you here," he said. "With me, where you belong. So we can be together."

"That's not possible and you know it. Besides, I'm going to Paris in June. With Victor."

"Are you sure about that?"

There was something sinister in Dario's voice that caused Adam's heart to race. It felt like the wine cellar was suddenly swallowing him whole. "What do you mean by that?"

"I took care of it," he said.

Adam couldn't hide the anxiousness in his words. "Took care of what?"

"What day is it?" Dario asked. "The date? If it were that important, you would know."

Adam licked his lips. They felt dry and cracked. He wanted air. "I *don't* know."

Adam realized the answer before Dario even spoke. Hearing the words he was dreading only set his adrenaline into motion. "It's the first of March," he whispered in Adam's ear. "You know what that means. It's all over now. You're all mine."

"No...it can't be," Adam insisted. "I've been busy. *You've* kept me busy."

"Not busy enough," Dario said. "You should be taking care of me. My needs. Things are going to be different from now on. Between you and me. You're going to do exactly what I say. No more of this playing-hard-to-get nonsense. You're not a child, Adam. Stop acting like one."

Fuck you.

"He wouldn't leave me behind," Adam said. "He would never leave without saying good-bye. You don't know him like I do. Victor wouldn't—"

Dario turned Adam around with tremendous force, causing him to smack his forehead against the wooden beam. His face started to throb with pain. He felt dizzy and disoriented.

What is happening to me? He almost knocked me out.

"I made sure of it," Dario said. "Victor was on the first plane this morning. An anonymous gift arrived to his apartment via messenger. He agreed to leave early in exchange for a first class ticket and ten thousand dollars in cash."

"I don't believe you," said Adam. "Victor wouldn't do that. He's not like you."

"Go to Chicago. Find out for yourself."

Adam's voice rose. His anger couldn't be contained. "Why would you do something like this?"

"I don't like having competition."

"But there is none, Dario. There never will be."

"Not anymore," Dario agreed. "I'm all you have now."

Dario reached around the front of Adam's body and unbuttoned his jeans with one fast tug.

"Please don't do this to me."

"You almost sound scared," Dario said. "I like that. I like people to fear me." He pulled down Adam's pants. He reached down and spread Adam's cheeks apart. "Look at that sweet hole. It's begging for my cock."

There was a wine bottle sitting on top of a nearby barrel.

"You act like some uptight little virgin," Dario said. He spat in his hand and rubbed it over the head of his cock.

Adam reached for the wine bottle. "I am, actually."

Dario's breath quickened. "Oh yeah?"

Adam's palm wrapped around the neck of the wine bottle. He lifted the bottle as he spoke. "But I'm sorry, Dario. My first time will *not* be with you."

Instead of using it as weapon, Adam threw the bottle with every ounce of strength he had. It shattered into several pieces against the wall.

The sound of the breaking glass was so loud. Someone had to hear it. Someone will help me.

Adam glanced up to the low ceiling of the wine cellar. He heard footsteps above them. They were moving fast, and there were a lot of them.

Now the door is opening. I'm going to be free.

Before Dario had the chance to pull his pants back up or step away from Adam, the dinner guests were standing in the doorway, crowded together shoulder to shoulder.

Adam looked up at the curious eyes peering down at them. There was Evangelina. And Jane. And even Anastasia was there, pushing her way through the crowd.

As a brass key slipped from Evangelina's hand and hit the wooden first step, Adam reached down and pulled up his jeans and buttoned them quickly.

His voice cracked as he spoke, the words loud enough for everyone to hear: "By the way…I quit."

He moved away from Dario and walked up the creaking stairs, holding his head up high. He made eye contact with Evangelina for a brief second. "He's all yours," he said.

The crowd parted as if Adam were contagious. They scrambled to get out of his way.

Adam moved through the house quickly, aware someone was following him. He could hear the footsteps echoing behind him on the white marble floor of the foyer.

Then the sweet voice spoke. And the sound broke Adam's heart.

"He tried to make you do it, didn't he? And now you'll go away," she said. "I hate him."

Adam turned and looked down into Anastasia's fire-filled eyes. "I'm sorry you had to see that," he said. "You have no idea how truly sorry I am."

"But you said no," she said. "Didn't you? I can tell. You said no to him. No one's ever done that before."

"I have to go, Anastasia."

She lowered her stare. "I know."

"And I'm not coming back."

Her eyes filled with tears. "They never do."

Adam touched her cheek with the back of his fingers. "I want you to do me a favor," he said. "Be different. Don't become them."

"Take me with you," she begged.

Adam turned away. He moved to the double front doors. "I can't do that and you know it," he said. "This is where you belong."

Her words stopped him. "We both know that's not true," she said.

"Then tell your story," he said over his shoulder. He opened the door and breathed in the icy air. "Tell everyone the truth."

Her voice was defiant and determined. "Oh, I will," she promised, "Every word of it."

❖

Adam slid into the backseat of the smoky cab. Nancy Sinatra was singing a song on the radio.

Bang. Bang.

"You okay?" Myrtle asked. She straightened her white visor and put the cab into drive.

Adam nodded. "I will be," he said. "For now, let's get out of here."

Myrtle pulled away from the Vassalo mansion.

Adam stared through the glass. He could see Anastasia standing in the window of the formal living room. She looked like a living doll in her green party dress and long dark hair. With both palms pressed against the windowpanes, she looked trapped. She was a figurine desperate to escape the confines of her music box home, where the same haunting melody played over and over.

As Myrtle guided them through the snow-beaten roads to the train station, Adam fished his cell phone out of his coat pocket. He dialed Victor's number. The call went straight to voice mail.

Hi. This is Victor. I'll be out of the country for a while…

Adam closed his eyes and fought back an instant wave of tears.

No. What have I done? How could I have forgotten about the date?

Adam tucked his phone away as they arrived at the station.

Myrtle found his eyes in the rearview mirror.

"Listen, I don't know what happened back there but you're a good kid," she said. "Do whatever you can to stay that way."

❖

Adam got on the train. Sitting alone and staring out the window, he could still smell Dario on his skin.

I'm permanently stained. He's all over me.

Adam thought about Evangelina. Less than a half hour ago, she was sitting at the head of the formal dining table in her beautiful evening gown. When did she realize that just below her feet in the wine cellar, her husband was forcing himself on their daughter's tutor? What did she say to her guests in the aftermath? How did she handle the humiliation of what they all saw?

Did Anastasia really know what her father was capable of? Had she seen something like this before? How long would it be before she had another new tutor?

I need to tell someone about the wall. The police.

Adam didn't even realize he was crying. He wiped his eyes with the back of his hand and prayed all the way to Chicago that Victor had changed his mind.

That somehow, he'd still be there.

Waiting.

CHAPTER NINE

A dam started his frantic search at Victor's lakeside apartment. He rang the buzzer. He waited. He rang again. He considered scaling the fire escape and prying open a window. He thought about yelling Victor's name at the top of his lungs.

Finally, a brunette in a low-cut blouse emerged from the building. Adam nearly pushed her out of the way to get inside. He took the stairs two at a time.

He was in the middle of writing Victor a note when a door across the hall from Victor's studio apartment opened.

It was Victor's neighbor Rowena, the one he always complained about. He said she was always in everyone's business and filled her days with keeping track of the tenants' whereabouts. She was an elderly woman, short and thin. She was wearing a faded floral-patterned housecoat that was at least two sizes too large. On her feet were frayed pink slippers. Her stark white hair was a mess, as if she'd just woken up.

"You looking for the Mexican boy?" she asked. Her voice was kind and gentle.

"Yes. Have you seen him?"

"I have."

"Do you know where he is? It's very important."

"He moved out earlier today." she said.

"What do you mean he moved?"

"He's gone."

"Maybe you're wrong," Adam said.

She pulled a key out of the front pocket of her baggy dress. "The place is empty," she said. She shuffled her way to the lock on Victor's door. "Some movers came. I was suspicious because they looked like hoodlums. They said they were taking his things to a storage unit."

"Are you sure?"

"Here," she said, unlocking the door and pushing it open with her palm. "Take a look for yourself if you don't believe me. The landlord gave me a key to show it to people who come by. If you're interested in renting it, I can give you his telephone number. It's overpriced for a studio, if you ask me, but it's got a great view of the lake. In fact, you can even see Navy Pier."

Adam stepped inside. Just as the old woman had said, the apartment was empty.

Crushed, Adam went home. There was no sign of Stacey either. The apartment was strangely quiet and unusually clean.

What is happening to my world? Everything is changing. I feel like I've landed on another planet. This looks like my life…but it can't be.

Adam plugged in his charger and connected his dead cell phone. He dialed Victor's number. The call went straight to voice mail. He tried again. And again.

Damn. What do I do?

Adam glanced around the apartment as if the answer would somehow reveal itself.

Find Stacey. Maybe Victor missed his plane. Maybe they're together talking about what an idiot you are. Maybe they're at the pub.

Adam showered quickly, scrubbing the smell of Dario Vassalo off his body once and for all. He watched with a sense of satisfaction as the water swirled down the drain.

I'm rid of you forever. You've ruined everything for me. I'm never going back there. I'm done. Once I find Victor, I can have my old life back.

Then everything will be normal again.

❖

Adam found her drunk and perched on a bar stool.

"Stacey, where's Victor?" She stared at him through half-closed eyes. She looked like a hippie in bell-bottom jeans and an embroidered peasant blouse. Her dark hair was bone straight. She had a daisy tucked behind one ear. The petals were starting to wilt.

"Where the fuck have you been?" Her words were slurred and slow. "We need to celebrate. Buy me a drink."

"You have to help me find him. Please."

"Who?"

He fought the impulse to shake her. "Victor!"

"Oh," she said. "*Him*. He just left. You just missed him. He said he's going to the airport."

"Which one?"

She had to think about it for a moment. "O'Hare," she said. "His flight leaves at midnight. So…ya better hurry."

Thank God. There's still time. Go.

Adam darted out of the pub and ran to the closest train station. He jumped on the Blue Line heading to O'Hare Airport.

He sat down in a seat on the almost-empty train and tried to catch his breath. He dialed Victor's number.

Voice mail. Again. *Fuck it. I'm leaving him a message. What choice do I have?*

"Victor," he said, still breathless. "It's Adam. Listen to me. You can't get on that plane. Please. I'm on my way to the airport."

Adam started to cry. He closed his eyes and remembered.

"I love you," he said. "Please don't go."

❖

Minutes later, Adam was standing in the airport searching the overhead monitor screens for a departing red-eye flight to Paris. He felt motionless, staring up and standing still while hurried strangers passed him by, moving around him like he was invisible.

His cell phone rang. He could feel it buzzing in the front pocket of his jeans. He recognized the picture on the screen, the number.

"Victor?"

"Adam?"

"Oh, thank God," Adam said. His entire body began to tremble. "Where are you?"

"I'm on the plane. We're about to take off. I just got your message."

No. This can't be happening. I'm so close to reaching him. "Listen to me. I don't what you've been told, but it's not true."

"Are you sure?" Victor said. "The man who came to see me was very clear. He said you made up your mind. He said you didn't want to see me anymore and that I shouldn't even bother contacting you. I was supposed to be on a flight this morning…but I waited."

"He was lying to you."

"Why would he do that?" Victor asked.

"I can't explain that right now. There isn't enough time. I'm here. I'm in the airport looking for you."

"You came here for me?"

"Yes," Adam said. "To get you. To stop you. To tell you—"

"Tell me?" he said. "Tell me what?"

Adam tried to swallow the wave of tears rising up. He lost the battle. "To tell you that I love you."

"Adam?" he said. "Are you crying?"

"Yes, damn it," he said. "Because I don't want you to go. We're supposed to be together and we both know it. You can't leave, Victor. Not like this."

"The only thing that matters to me is you, Adam. I know you love me," he said. "And I love you, too."

Relief flooded Adam. Tears continued to fill his eyes. "You have no idea how good it is to hear you say that. I've missed you. Everything about you. Your voice. Your smile. I've been such an idiot."

"Yes, you have," Victor said. "But I forgive you."

"I got lost," said Adam.

"On the way to the airport?"

"No," he said. "On my way to you. I got detoured by my own stupid fears."

"You wouldn't be you if you were perfect," he said. "I have to go, Adam."

"Don't say that," Adam said. "I just want to hold you. I need to be with you right now."

Adam could hear the smile in Victor's voice. "You are."

"What are we going to do?"

"You're going to graduate. I'm going to find us an apartment."

"I will meet you in Paris as soon as I can."

"It's a date," he said. "I'd wait for you forever if I had to."

"It won't be that long," Adam said. "I'll be there in June."

"I hope you don't mind, but I plan on stalking you every second we're apart," said Victor.

Adam wiped his eyes. He grinned. "I wouldn't have it any other way," he said. "Please text me or call me when you get there."

"I will see you in…" Victor's voice started to fade in and out.

"I can't hear you. You're breaking up on me." Adam gripped his phone tighter. "Victor?"

He was gone.

Within seconds, the phone rang again. But it wasn't Victor.

"Mom?" Adam said. "What's going on?"

Becca took a deep breath before she spoke. "I'm at the hospital," she said. "Your grandfather is dying. You need to get here as fast as you can."

Adam closed his eyes and whispered a silent prayer. "I'm on my way."

He turned around and headed back to the train station.

CHAPTER TEN

A dam saw his grandmother the second the elevator doors opened. She was sitting in a row of chairs. With her flaming auburn hair, excessive jewelry, and high heels some women wouldn't dare to wear, she looked terribly out of place in such a sterile environment.

She stood up to greet Adam. She moved like her arms were weighing her down, like her entire body was too heavy to maneuver. Her attempt to hug him seemed awkward and forced.

"You're too late," she whispered into his ear.

"Nana?" Adam tried to pull away but his grandmother wouldn't let go. She started to cry. Adam could feel her body shake with sobs. She clung to him.

I've never seen her cry before. She's always been so strong. Suddenly, she's falling apart in my arms.

"He's gone, Adam," she said.

She let go.

"What happened?" Adam asked, barely able to breathe. The walls of the dingy county hospital corridor felt like they were closing in. Soon, he and Nana would be crushed.

I hate this place.

She moved back to her chair but instead of sitting down,

she just stared at it as if someone had stolen her seat. "He had a stroke," she said to the empty space she'd occupied when Adam had arrived.

Adam was nervous. His body was surging with a strange, jittery energy. He started to pace because he had to move. He had to do *something*. "But…people recover from strokes. I know they do. It happens all the time."

Nana shook her head. She reached into her designer bag for a tissue. She dabbed at the corner of her eyes, careful not to smudge her mascara or touch the thick tips of her false eyelashes. "He slipped into a coma because of it. It happened so fast."

"They couldn't bring him back?"

"They tried," she said. "They did everything they could, but the son of a bitch gave up and died."

"Grandpa's really dead?"

Adam heard his mother's voice before he saw her. It came from behind him. "He loved you very much, Adam."

He turned. Becca was standing in the center of the hallway, clutching two paper cups of coffee. She had her pocketbook tucked underneath her arm. Her eyes were bloodshot and her nose red. She was still dressed for work in a black and white tweed pantsuit.

She's my mother. She's beautiful just the way she is. She's been so alone for all these years. What would I do if something happened to Victor?

"I know he did, Mom," he said. "He loved all of us."

Nana was on her feet. Her voice rose and bounced off the white walls of the stark corridor. "He nearly killed himself trying to take care of you," she said to Becca.

"Now isn't the time for one of your guilt trips, Vivian," Adam's mother said. She handed Nana one of the cups of coffee. "Drink it."

"How?" Nana said. "How is that possible? The only thing that'll make me feel better just died."

"Don't worry," Becca said. "I'll help you...take care of everything. We're family."

Nana sniffed the coffee, gave a look of disgust, and dumped it into a trash can. "We both know how much you leaned on him for help," she said. "Constantly."

"What else did you expect me to do? I was all alone. You know that."

Nana moved to the elevator. She pushed the button with a quick jab of her index finger. "You could've found another man," she said. "Women do it all the time. People move on, Becca."

Becca followed her. They were face-to-face, eye to eye. "I found the perfect one twenty-three years ago," his mother said. "Your son. Remember him? But he took a wrong step and got killed in a minefield. It was an accident. People die, Vivian, whether we want them to or not."

The elevator doors opened. "Why didn't you just remarry?" Nana asked.

To Adam's surprise, his mother was the one who stepped inside. *She* was leaving. "Because even though I was only eighteen, I made a promise I would *never* love someone else," she said. "And I kept it."

The silver doors slid shut.

❖

"I should've gone to the airport," Becca said an hour later. They were sitting in the Granny Mobile, parked at the curb outside Adam's apartment building. Adam had followed his mother and found her in the hospital parking lot, searching for her car in the cold. She insisted on driving him home. The temperature was below freezing, so Adam accepted the offer for a ride. En route, they stopped at a drive-thru window, ordered some food, and spoke in short sentences about nothing. After pulling into the only empty spot on the block, they sat in silence.

Until now.

"What for?" Adam asked.

He breathed in deep, fighting back another wave of emotion. The interior of the car smelled like French fries. He reached for his large soda and brought the straw to his mouth.

"To say good-bye to Victor," his mother said.

Adam remembered Victor was gone. Hearing the words made it all the more real. It would be over three months until he would see him again.

"I owed him that much," she added.

Why is she sounding so cryptic? She's hiding something from me. I can tell. I can always tell. When will this horrible evening come to an end?

Adam gave his mother a strange look. "What are you talking about, Mom? You don't owe Victor anything."

She shook her head. The movement was slow and gentle. "But I do."

"Just because he and I finally came to our senses and he's taking me off your hands?" Adam tried to make a joke because the energy between them felt strange and he knew they needed to laugh. But Becca didn't even crack a smile. She kept staring through the windshield at the street lamp on the corner as if she were on the verge of slipping into a catatonic state for good. "He only wants to be with me because he knows you're gonna be one helluva mother-in-law. Really, none of this has anything to do with me. He just wants to be related to you."

I miss you already. I can't wait to be with you. To start our life together. Finally.

"His brother came to see me," his mother said. "That day."

The silence returned, blanketing the air around them and creating a sudden, eerie hush.

Adam's voice cracked when he finally spoke. His words cut through the heavy, overheated air in the car. "What?"

"Lorenzo came to the bank, Adam," she said. "He came inside and he found me."

"What are you talking about? You saw him before he got shot?"

"I was standing at the vending machine," she said. "He walked up to me and asked if I was your mother. I said yes. He explained to me who he was because we'd never met. He said Victor told him I was a good person. That I was like a second mother to him."

"You are, Mom. You look out for all of us. Even Stacey."

"Lorenzo said he needed help. He almost started to cry. I could see how frightened he was. Some people were coming after him. He said he owed them some money. So I asked him how much. He told me he needed a hundred and twenty dollars."

"That's it?"

"But instead of the cash or a hug, I gave him a lecture. I told him he needed to make better choices for himself. I said he needed to be more like his brother. When I told him I wasn't going to give him the money, he looked at me and said something strange…like *nothing matters anymore.*"

"What were you supposed to do? Mom, it wasn't your fault. It had nothing to do with you. He was mixed up in a bad situation."

"But I was his last hope," she said. Tears fell from her eyes and trickled down her cheeks. "I let him walk outside, Adam. I let him go out there unprotected."

"There was nothing you could've done," he said. "There's no way you could've stopped it, Mom."

"They were waiting for him in a car across the street. They shot him five times. Just to make sure he was dead."

Becca started to sob. She was so overwhelmed by her grief and the memory and her tears, it was difficult to understand her words. "They told us not to go outside. They locked down the bank."

Adam turned and looked out the passenger window of his mother's oversized car. He studied the cracks in the sidewalk. He noticed there was no snow. Maybe spring was coming early. God, he hoped so. "I remember," he said. "You called me."

"You're right, Adam. There was nothing I could do. I couldn't save him even though I wanted to. I watched him bleed to death on the sidewalk through the door. The bank manager kept telling me to get away from the windows. Stay away from the glass. I refused until they dragged me away. Then I heard the sirens."

"Mom, why didn't you ever tell me this?"

"Because I buried it away. I had to."

"Why bring it up now? Victor's halfway to Paris. He doesn't even talk to his sister or his mother anymore. You know that."

"We're all he has," she said. "Every time I look into Victor's eyes I'm reminded of that horrible afternoon. And of his brother's last words to me. He said, 'If something happens to me, make sure my brother is all right. I think he just needs someone to love.' And now, he has that." Becca took a breath. "He has you."

I just want to go. I want to go upstairs and take a hot shower. I want to curl up on the sofa and forget about death and airplanes. I want to laugh again. I want to be with Victor.

"No matter what, I will help get you to Paris," his mother promised.

"Then you might need to help me find a job," he said.

She turned to him then. He could feel her eyes on him. "What happened?"

"It's a long story, but I don't work for the Vassalo family anymore."

"Adam, what did you do?" Becca's cell phone rang. She reached into her purse sitting between them. "Is it something we can fix?"

"No," he said. "In fact, I never want to go back there again."

"Hello?" she said. A sense of fear crept into the car. Adam could feel it immediately. It chilled him. Then he heard his mother's words, and by her tone, he knew she was afraid. "Joe? How did you get this number?"

Adam's phone buzzed. He reached into the front pocket of his jeans to retrieve it. A text. *Can Victor already be in Paris? Is that even possible? What time is it?*

The text was from Dario. Adam stared at the words on the screen of his cell. They set off a second round of anxiousness, triggering a cold sweat.

I have to see you. Tomorrow. Be here at noon.

Then another text came through.

Or else.

CHAPTER ELEVEN

Myrtle Brubaker was standing beside her cab outside the Lake Bluff Metra train station. She was dressed in her usual pastel-colored style: purple windbreaker, lemon yellow polyester slacks, stark white sneakers, and the white visor that seemed permanently attached to her forehead. Her blue-tinted hair was unusually bright. Adam wondered if she was just returning from an appointment at a nearby beauty parlor.

It feels like so much time has passed since I first arrived in this town. Everything has happened so fast. Thank God for Myrtle. She's the only person I've met around here who makes any sense.

"Hey, kid," she said once he was in earshot. She spat the shell of a sunflower seed out on the sidewalk. "Didn't think I'd ever see ya again."

"I almost didn't make it, Myrtle," he said. "The weather in the city was bad. Most of the trains are delayed."

"That storm's heading this way," she said. "Heard it mahself on the radio. We better get a move on. I don't wantcha getting stuck out here."

"That makes two of us."

Myrtle climbed in behind the steering wheel and turned

down the stereo. Adam slid in to the backseat and pulled the door closed. He could hear Nancy Sinatra's voice. It was faint but he knew she was singing her signature tune.

These boots are made for walking. That's sound advice indeed, Nancy. Once I have the chance to tell this man face-to-face what I think of him, I will turn around and walk away. For good.

"He musta promised you the moon to get ya to come back up here," she said.

"He and I have some unfinished business to take care of, it seems," Adam said.

I want to get a closer look at the wall in the wine cellar before I go to the police. I want to be sure.

"Well, you say your piece and then I'll take you back to the station."

"Fair enough."

"I know it's none of my business, but I'm real happy to see you're moving on."

"I am," he said. "As soon as I'm finished with school, I'm going to Paris."

"Good for you," she said. "For your sake, I hope you make it there."

Adam leaned forward a little. He stared at the back of Myrtle's overprocessed hair. "I don't know how to thank you, Myrtle."

"Thank me?" she said. "I did my job, kid. You don't owe me nothin' for that."

"My grandfather died last night," he said. "I didn't get to say good-bye to him."

"Damn, I'm real sorry to hear that. I know he meant a lot to you."

"So do you," he said. "I'm sure that sounds strange, but after last night and everything that's happened in my life lately, I feel like I need to let you know that I appreciate you."

"Well, that's nice of ya to say, but don't go expectin' me to get all soft on ya. That's just not my style."

"I know," he said. "That's why I like you."

Moments later, Myrtle turned onto the paved private road. Adam looked up to the towering pine trees. The sky was darkening. Storm clouds were rolling in. And fast.

"This shouldn't take long," he said.

"You never know," she said. "He might convince you to stay, kid. From what I hear, he can be pretty persuasive when he wants something real bad."

Myrtle pulled up in front of the castle-styled Tudor mansion. Adam stared in awe through the window, remembering the first time he'd arrived.

"This place still scares me," he said.

"It looks haunted, if you ask me."

"I'm pretty sure it is," Adam said.

"I hear they've got twelve bedrooms and seven bathrooms in there."

"It's true," said Adam, not sure if he was telling the truth.

"What does somebody need all those rooms for?"

Adam thought about Anastasia. "To get lost if you need to."

Myrtle shook her head. "I don't care how much money I might have, this place would never feel like home to me. I'll take my little apartment any day. It might not be much, but at least I know where everything is."

"You're right," he said.

Myrtle reached for her bag of sunflower seeds in the seat beside her and said, "Money can't buy everything."

❖

Adam rang the doorbell and waited for Jane to appear. When that didn't happen, he rang again. And again.

His phone buzzed. A text message.

Come in. I'm waiting for you in the library.

Sure enough, the front doors were unlocked. Adam turned the giant knobs, pushed the doors open with both hands, and closed them behind him.

Except for the constant ticking of the grandfather clock, the house seemed strangely quiet and even larger than Adam remembered. He felt incredibly alone.

Let's get this over with.

He entered the library. There was no sign of Dario. He stepped farther into the room. Through the window, he could see Myrtle waiting dutifully in her cab.

"I'm the one who asked you here."

Adam knew who the voice belonged to before he turned around, but he turned anyway, just to make sure he was right.

Evangelina stood in the center of the room in a green sweater and gray slacks. Her dark auburn hair was half up and her skin looked as radiant and flawless as ever. She was wearing diamond stud earrings that matched her wedding ring.

"Why would you do that?" he asked. "Send me a text pretending to be your husband? That doesn't seem like your style, Mrs. Vassalo. Aren't you the one who told me to disappear? Why bring me back?"

She took a step toward him. "I did it because I think you and I need to have another talk," she said. "I wanted to tell you…face-to-face. Adam, there are more things you should know."

He looked into her eyes and said, "I know enough to leave."

Adam moved toward the double-sized open doorway of the room. Her words stopped him in his tracks. "You're not the only one."

He looked back. She'd moved and was now standing in front of the fireplace. There were only embers left, the remnants of an earlier blaze that was dying out. "You're leaving Dario?" he asked, hearing the hope in his own voice.

"I was planning to, yes," she said. "Seeing the two of you…*together* was the last straw for me. I don't think I've ever been angrier in my life."

"I don't blame you," he said. "I'd be angry too if I were you."

"But I'm afraid my husband beat me to it."

"What do you mean?"

"He got up early this morning," she said. "He went to Chicago and had breakfast with his lawyer. He filed for divorce. The papers arrived an hour before you did."

Adam was at a loss for words. All he could get out was "I'm sorry."

Evangelina gave him a look. It was an angry smile. "What for? Because you're young and attractive? Because my husband wanted you so badly he brought you into our home? Because I'm a woman, my husband will never look at me the same way he looks at you? Is *that* what you're apologizing for?"

"I'm sorry for what's happened to you," he said. "You don't deserve this."

"None of us do," she said. "After he left his attorney's

office, he went to the airport. He got on a plane to God knows where. I only know this because he had the decency to send me a text message."

"Business trip?"

She folded her arms across her chest. "You tell me."

"I don't understand what you want. Why did you trick me into coming here?"

"I had to send you that text last night and pretend to be Dario, otherwise I knew you wouldn't come back."

"Well, I'm here now," he said. "And I'd like to leave soon."

"I've told you about the other young men," she said. "Even the boy who went missing. Not once did I get the chance to speak to any of them alone, to hear it for myself. What he does to you."

Have you checked the wine cellar? I'm pretty sure Charlie Bower is buried behind the wall down there. Maybe your husband has more secrets than either of us will ever know about.

"There's nothing to tell, Evangelina," he said, avoiding the pleading look in her eyes. She wanted answers. "I need to get back to Chicago."

"Do you know where my husband is, Adam?"

"No," he said "How could I?"

"He hasn't contacted you?"

"I think there's a misunderstanding."

"Is there?" she said, holding his gaze. "What am I not getting? Explain it to me."

"I was never *with* your husband. Believe whatever you want, but there was no affair."

"Please remember this is still my house and I'm still Evangelina Vassalo. Do not disrespect me or what I've been through for the sake of my marriage by lying to me."

"I've never lied to you," he said. "I came here because I needed a job. I told you that."

"You came here because my husband *created* a job for you. Because he wanted you."

"I didn't realize that until later."

"When did the thought occur to you? When I caught him sneaking out of the guest room or when my dinner guests and I found you both with your pants down in the wine cellar?"

"I never had sex with your husband."

She took a breath. "I almost believe you."

"Well, you should. You know what he's like."

She nodded gently. "I'm afraid I do."

"I'm in love with someone else. I have been since before I came here. I told you this. It's not a lie."

Evangelina looked confused. "Did you tell this to Dario?"

"Of course I did. But he didn't take it very well."

"I can only imagine," she said. "My husband isn't used to being told no."

"You don't know the half of it. He interfered. He offered the man I love ten thousand dollars to walk away and never see me again."

"I know what my husband will do to win," she said.

Do you? Do you really?

"I think this is just a game to Dario. He likes the thrill of being bad. He likes being sneaky and wondering if he's going to get caught."

"And you don't?"

"Honestly, I just needed to pay my rent," Adam said. "I don't come from much. My dad died before I was born. It was just me and my mom and my grandpa and Nana while I was growing up. But we just lost my grandfather. Victor is in Paris waiting for me to start our life together, but the soonest I can get there is June. And I feel like the only person I can talk to is Myrtle."

Evangelina's posture tensed. "Myrtle has been very good to me." She made a face. "He said he was in love with *you*," she said. "My husband. After you left last night, I confronted him. I asked him for the truth and he admitted his feelings for you."

"Is that why he left?"

"He left because you destroyed him," she said. "I could see it the moment you walked out the door. When he realized you were never coming back. He knows he lost. You won, Mr. Parsh."

"Me?" he said. "I don't have the power to destroy a man like Dario."

"But you did," she said. "Because you are the one thing in this world he can't have."

"And he never will," Adam said. "That much I promise you."

Evangelina sat down in the cream-colored love seat in front of the potted palm.

"Do you have any idea what I've been through because of him, what I've given up?" she said. Adam shook his head. She gestured to the matching love seat opposite hers. Adam took his cue to sit and listen. "I had a successful career in Greece. I was a doctor. I had my own practice. I could've retired years ago if I'd stayed in Athens. While I was still young enough to enjoy it all. I had a beautiful life there. My friends. My family. But fifteen years ago, I met Dario Vassalo. Our fathers are both in politics. They're both members of the Greek Parliament, so it made sense for us to date and fall in love and get married. He asked me and of course, I said yes. Many people benefited from our marriage. Our families merged and we were given incredible wealth and power. Dario was smart. He made a lot of money very fast in Greece."

"But were you in love? When you married him, I mean?"

"No," she said. "I was in lust. He was very attractive. He was a good lover. He spoiled me and gave me everything I ever wanted."

"That seems to be his style."

"A year after we were married, he came to me and told me we were moving to the States. At first, I refused. Greece is my home and it always will be. But in the end, he won. I got on the plane. A few weeks after we arrived, I had a meeting with the board of our local hospital. They decided my credentials from Greece weren't good enough. I could be a doctor in America, but only if I went back to school. When I told them no, they offered me a position as a nurse in the emergency room. The only reason I took the job was because I like to work. I love to help people and save them. But Dario would only allow me to work part-time. He said I needed to be available for business trips and dinner parties and basically to serve as his perfect wife," she said. "And I hated him because of it. Soon, I realized the truth about him and who he really is. His secret."

"Why didn't you just leave him and go back to Greece?" Adam asked.

"I stayed because of Anastasia."

"And now?"

"Dario Vassalo is the biggest regret of my life. Now I have to sell this house. I have to pack what we want and get rid of the rest. I have to go somewhere and start all over again. I need to make a new life for my daughter and me.

And then there's Jane. She's been with us for so long, I don't know what she'll do now."

"Where is she?" he asked. "Is she here? I want her to tell me more about Charlie Bower. What she saw."

"Some secrets are better left unspoken," she said. "Let's leave Jane out of this. I asked her to meet Anastasia at school and take her out for the afternoon. I figured it would be best if we had this conversation alone. I planned to give you a piece of my mind and shame you for your relations with my husband. But you're just a young man who got mixed up with the wrong family."

"I'm no saint, Evangelina," he said. "I thought about having an affair with him. God knows he was very convincing."

"I'm sure he was. I know from experience…you're his type."

"But I couldn't do that to you…or to Victor. Even though Dario said the two of you have an arrangement."

She looked away. "The arrangement is simple," she said. "He does what he wants and he expects me to turn a blind eye. I've tried my best to do that, but after seeing the two of you together…but it's over now." Her cell phone rang. She answered it. "Hello?"

Adam's eyes drifted around the room to the floor-to-ceiling shelves of books.

I wonder if they're even real. Maybe they're just a prop. They're fake like everything else in this ridiculous house.

Evangelina was finished with her call. "I have some news," she said.

Adam looked up. "About Dario?"

She nodded. "My source says he's on his way to Greece," she said. "It seems he decided to go back home."

"Without even telling you?" Adam asked. "What about Anastasia? I mean, how can he leave the country without even saying good-bye to his own daughter?"

"He'll feel bad later," she said. "And when he does, my daughter will benefit greatly from his guilt. Maybe I will, too."

"You don't seem surprised," Adam said. "That he's going back to Greece."

"He loves the country even more than I do," she said. "If I know my husband, he'll go to Ios. It's the island where he was born. Even though his mother is dead, he believes her spirit is still there. And they were very close."

Outside, Adam heard the familiar squeal of old brakes followed by the closing of a car door. The sound created a tickle of fear inside him. Immediately, he sensed something was wrong. He could feel it invade the air around them, the presence of danger.

"Is someone here?" Evangelina asked. She stood up and went to the window. Adam followed.

He recognized the beast of a car at once. The Granny Mobile was parked next to Myrtle's cab. "It's my mother," Adam said.

"Maybe she's been trying to reach you."

"Where's my phone?" He searched his coat pockets, but it wasn't there. He fished it out of the front pocket of his jeans. "Damn it. I turned it off on the train ride up here and forgot to turn it back on."

There was a frantic pounding on the front door. Evangelina moved into the foyer. Adam remained where he was. He tried desperately to dismiss the gnawing sense of dread that felt as if it were eating him alive. He went to the framed photo of Dario on a yacht, the photo that had caught his eye weeks ago during his first meeting with Evangelina.

It's strange. After what I know about you now, you don't seem so irresistible to me anymore. I'm glad I never gave in to you. You're a monster.

Becca entered the room wide-eyed and panicked. "Oh, thank God!"

Adam couldn't remember seeing his mother so worried before. She was frightened. "Mom? What's the matter? What are you doing here? Is it Nana?"

"No," she said. "It's Joe."

Is she insane?

"Who in the hell is Joe? We don't know anyone named Joe."

"The customer," she stammered. "The restraining order."

"Have you lost your mind? You came all the way here because of—"

Becca placed a palm over her heart. She was struggling to catch her breath. "He threatened to kill us."

Adam's heart began to race. Beads of sweat formed on the back of his neck and behind his ears. "What?"

Evangelina lifted her cell phone and started to dial. "Do I need to call the police?"

"I already have," Becca explained. "They're looking for him."

"They don't know where he is?" Adam asked.

Evangelina looked genuinely scared. "Why would this man threaten you?"

"Mrs. Vassalo, it's not just me he's upset with," Becca said. "He also wants to harm your husband."

"What for? What has Dario done now?"

"This man has lost everything and he blames us."

"And that's a good enough reason to threaten to kill someone?" Evangelina said. "What is this world coming to?"

Adam reached for his mother's hand. "Mom, let's go," he said. "There's no sense in staying here and putting Mrs. Vassalo in danger."

Fear filled Evangelina's eyes. "Wait," she said. "I hear a car."

The three of them rushed to the window. They stood, shoulder to shoulder, peering through the glass.

"Maybe it's Myrtle," Adam said.

Evangelina stepped away from the window as if it were on fire. "It's not her. I don't recognize the car. It's a man."

Becca was on the verge of tears. "Oh my God, what if he followed me here?"

"Why would he do that?" Adam asked.

Evangelina sprang into action. "Help me close the drapes. I don't want him to see us."

Becca obeyed the command and pulled one side of the thick drapes closed, shrouding her half of the window. Evangelina did the same on the other side. The room darkened.

"Adam, call the police," his mother instructed. "Tell them to get here."

"My phone is off." He pushed a button to turn it on.

"I'll call them," Evangelina said. She dialed and put her cell phone to her ear.

"Do you have a security system in the house?" Becca asked.

"Of course we do. I just have no idea how to use it."

"Do you have a gun?"

"I'm sure my husband does, but I don't know where he keeps it."

"Is there anyone else in the house?" asked Becca.

"No, just us," she said. Evangelina turned to Becca and gripped her arm. "Oh no. The front door."

The terror in the room was contagious. "What do you mean?"

"I let you in the front door," she said. "Did I lock it?"

A man with a gun in his hand walked into the room. "Apparently, you didn't," he said. He was nervous. He was shaking. Sweat trickled down the sides of his face. There was a crazed look in his eyes, mixing wildly with the sadness that was also in his intense gaze. "This was easier than I thought it would be. I just walked in. Right through the front door."

Adam stared at Joe. He looked like someone's young father in a pair of sweatpants, baseball cap, ratty sneakers, and a faded yellow T-shirt. He was a Little League coach. He was the guy who always volunteered to man the grill at neighborhood cookouts. He was the sensitive male friend who always knew the right thing to say to make you feel better.

Becca stepped in front of Evangelina and her son, shielding them with her body. "What do you want from us?" she asked.

"The police are looking for you," Evangelina said. "They'll be here any second."

He raised the gun. "I'm sure we'll all be dead by the time they get here."

Evangelina refused to be intimidated. "Is this some kind of sick joke to you?"

"You call losing your house and your job and being

forced to live out of your car a joke? You have no fucking idea what I've been through, lady. Do you live here? Is this your palace? Do you know what happened to me and my wife this morning? They took our children away from us."

"That has nothing to do with anyone in this room," Becca said. "What's happened to you isn't our fault, Joe."

"Do you believe in coincidences?" he asked. "Do you believe in fate? You said on the phone you had to go because you had a meeting with Dario Vassalo."

"I did," Adam's mother said. "He never showed up. Then you called back."

"That's right I did. Because I realized who he was. He's the son of a bitch who designed the subdivision we lived in for over a decade before your bank decided to throw us out on the street."

Becca softened her tone. "Joe, I know you're upset. I know what you've been through. And I've done everything I can. You have to believe me."

He lowered the gun.

He's even more terrified than we are.

"You couldn't possibly know one thing about my life," he said. "You don't even return my calls. That's all I wanted…just someone to call me…But you didn't do that."

"I know you don't want to do this. You're a good man."

"You know what?" he said. "I used to be."

She moved closer to him. Adam held his breath. "I know about loss," his mother said. "My husband was killed in the Gulf War, Joe. He stepped on a land mine and got blown away. I never even got to say good-bye and I was only eighteen. His father, who took care of me and my son and did the best he could to help us, died yesterday. So please don't force me to bury another person I love. Please, Joe. I won't do it. I can't."

Joe started to weep then. "I want my house back, Becca. I want my family. And I want my life again."

She lowered her eyes. "I can't do that," she said.

He's going to shoot her.

"Well, then who in the hell can?" Joe raised the gun. On instinct, Adam took a step forward. Joe fired.

The bullet tore into Adam's left shoulder. He dropped to his knees, stunned. He slid to the floor.

As he fell, he saw Joe step out of the room and into the foyer.

Seconds later, there was a second shot.

But all Adam heard was their voices.

"He's bleeding!"

Mom? Can you hear me? What's happened to me?

"Hold on, Adam. Don't you dare die on me."

"I need you to help me, Becca. Are you listening? Look at me. I used to be a doctor."

"Oh, thank God. Tell me what to do."

The light in the room seemed like it was dimming. Adam could see Evangelina throwing open the drapes and ripping the sheer curtains away from the window. She balled up the material and pressed it against his open wound. She instructed Becca how to hold it in place, to apply constant pressure.

Mom, I can feel your hands. You're trying to save me. Just like you wanted to save Lorenzo on the sidewalk that day. But I won't die like he did. I promise.

Evangelina slipped out of the room. Adam could hear her high heels on the marble floor of the foyer. She was speaking to someone.

She's on the phone. She's getting help.

My God, Mom. Stop crying.

Somebody go downstairs. I think someone is buried behind the brick wall in the wine cellar. I think Dario Vassalo is a murderer. Maybe he wanted to kill me.

"Adam, talk to me. Please. Just say something. Anything. Oh God, this is all my fault. Just hold on. We're getting help." She leaned down closer and whispered in his ear. "I want you to pretend like none of this happened. That I never let you come here. I want you to *Rewind.* You always loved to win that game. And that's what I need you to do right now."

I wish I could, Mom. I wish I could stand up. I'd play Rewind. Just for you.

Evangelina was back in the room. "There's a problem," she said. "A storm just hit. An ambulance is on the way but they might have some trouble getting through."

"Then we need to do something. My son has been shot."

"We have two options. You and I can carry him into the kitchen and I can do my best to remove the bullet."

"You're talking about operating on him? Here?"

"I can do it," Evangelina insisted.

"What's the other option?" Becca asked.

Another voice entered the room and cracked through the haze in Adam's head. At once, he knew who it was: his savior.

"Don't worry about it. I got this," Myrtle Brubaker said. "Help me get him into the back of my cab."

"What about the snow?"

"I know these roads better than anyone," she said. "Besides, I ain't afraid of no storm."

Adam could sense Myrtle beside him. He glanced up

and saw the rim of her familiar white visor resting just above her old blue eyes.

"Hey there, kid. You took a hit for the Vassalos, did ya? That's all right. We'll take care of you. I'll even let you choose whatever song you wanna listen to on the way to hospital. Just as long as it's Nancy Sinatra."

Adam attempted a smile but his mouth ached. It was difficult to speak because his throat was so dry, but he managed to get the words out.

He reached for Myrtle's hand. He squeezed it gently and said, "Bang. Bang."

CHAPTER TWELVE

The Athens airport was crowded and hot. Adam felt like he was in a daze as he moved through the throng of sweaty strangers. The flight had been long. Every hour of it seemed to have taken a toll on his body. All he wanted was a hot bath and a decent night's sleep in a decent bed.

What hour is it? What day is it? I'm starving.

There was no need to stop at baggage claim. He'd only brought a carry-on bag. Back in Chicago, he'd shipped most of his belongings to Paris.

You're two days away from Paris. From seeing the love of your life.

I'm on my way, Victor. But first, there's something I must do.

Outside, the evening air was cool and refreshing. Adam stood still for a moment, allowing the light breeze to tickle his skin. He closed his eyes and thought of freedom.

Finally, I will be rid of you once and for all.

Adam hailed a cab. He gave the driver the address of the hotel in Omonia Square Evangelina had recommended. In the backseat, he stared through the window at the sights of Athens, admiring the combination of classic and cutting-edge architecture. He wished Myrtle Brubaker was with him to see it. But she was busy with her new job. Soon enough, she'd get the chance to travel the world with Evangelina at her side.

She's been good to Myrtle. To all of us.

The clock on the dashboard of the cab revealed it was after midnight. Adam stifled a yawn. He reached into the outer zipper compartment of his carry-on bag and retrieved his cell phone. He pushed a button and waited for it to turn on.

Moments later, he sent a text to his mother.

I made it safely. I'm in Athens. Heading to the hotel. Love you.

He sent a second text to Stacey.

Congratulations, my friend. Ninety days sober is something to be proud of.

The third one was to Victor.

I can't wait to feel you next to me. Two days, my love.

Despite his state of exhaustion, Adam found it difficult to sleep. He tossed and turned, planning out each word he wanted to say. He rehearsed it over and over in his mind until the words started to tangle and blur.

Tomorrow, you'll finally be face-to-face.

He got up and opened the French doors leading out to a balcony. He caught a glimpse of the Athens skyline in the distance. The view gave him a deep sense of peace. He stood there, shirtless and sleepy, until he was fighting to keep his eyes open.

He crawled back into bed.

Adam tumbled head first into a heavy sleep weighed down by vivid dreams. The nightmares had ended just a few weeks ago.

When he woke a few hours later, he had to remind himself where he was and why. He climbed out of bed, took a quick shower, slipped into a black and white striped T-shirt, khaki shorts, and black Converse, and went downstairs with his carry-on in tow to check out of the hotel.

After grabbing a quick plate of fried potatoes and eggs and an orange Fanta at a nearby sidewalk café, he hailed a cab to the adjacent port city of Piraeus. There, he bought a ferry ticket to the island of Ios. He had a forty-five-minute wait until the ship departed, so he dashed into some of the souvenir shops and bought a few things, including a sweatshirt for Victor and a postcard to send to Nana with a picture on the front of it of a half-naked Greek guy.

Imagine her reaction when she goes to the mailbox. She'll probably thank me later.

Back outside, Adam approached the huge passenger boat that would take him across the Aegean Sea down to Ios in the Cyclades Islands.

There, he had a dinner date planned with Dario Vassalo.

❖

Dario was sitting at a table outside a café in the harbor. The sun was setting, casting a soft pink and orange glow over everything in its reachable path. The picturesque island looked alluring and romantic. It was a fantasy brought to life.

Dario was in dark sunglasses, a white short-sleeved shirt, khakis, and Italian leather shoes. He looked just as breathtaking as Adam remembered with his permanent five o'clock shadow, chiseled jawline, and thick, dark hair.

He raised his sunglasses, spotting Adam in the distance at once. Dario stood to greet him.

He still has that seductive power. But you know better now. You know what he's really like.

Adam felt a twinge of pain in his left shoulder when Dario slipped his arms around his body.

It's a reminder. So much has happened to so many people because of this man. You can't forget what's been done. My God, he still smells so good.

Adam sat down at the umbrella-covered table in a white plastic folding chair across from Dario.

As promised, Dario handed him an envelope. Adam peered inside. The money was American. Cash. A lot of it. He shoved the envelope into his pocket.

From across the table their eyes met. Dario grinned.

Adam leaned back in his chair. He felt his body start to relax. He'd been waiting for this moment for months, for the chance to tell Dario exactly what he thought of him face-to-face. He knew once it was over he'd be en route to his new life with Victor in Paris. This was just one last step in a very long journey.

The other tables at the quaint café were populated with tourists. A dozen different dialects and languages buzzed around Adam's head, creating an international cacophony. He tried his best to drown out their voices and remain focused on the task at hand.

As he imagined would happen, Adam spoke first. "I took a bullet that was meant for you, Dario." He tapped his left shoulder lightly. "Right here."

Dario lowered his eyes. "I should've been there," he said.

"But you weren't," Adam said. "You ran away. Why is that?"

"You really want to know?"

"More than anything."

"It's simple," he said. "I was scared, Adam. After that night in the wine cellar, I knew I'd lost you."

"But you never really had me to begin with," he said. "You know that. I kept telling you no. I was there in your house to do a job. You were my boss."

"But I knew you wanted me," he said. "And I can tell just by looking at you…you still do."

"Doesn't everybody?" Adam said. "You're no fool. You know what God's given you. The good looks. The money. The power. You could have anyone or anything in the world."

Dario folded his arms across his chest and leaned back in his chair. "Except for you," he said. "You've driven me crazy, Adam. I don't know how you've done it because nobody else ever has."

"It's the challenge, isn't it?" Adam said. "It's really not me at all. You just like the pursuit. You want to win."

"Haven't I?" he said. "You're here. We're together. In my country. I have much planned for you. This is just the beginning for us."

No, you smug fucker. This is the end. This is the moment where I stand up and walk off into the sunset.

Adam took a breath. He knew he needed to pace himself, otherwise he'd never get out all the words he wanted to say. "You don't know a thing about me except what you see. You couldn't care less about my family, my friends, how well I did in school, dreams I have for the future. Is it all just sex to you?"

"I find you very attractive," he said. "And I know you

feel the same about me. I felt it every time I touched you. I figure in due time I'll get to know you."

"I'm not an idiot, Dario," he said. "If I gave in to you and had the affair you wanted us to have, you'd toss me aside within weeks, if not days."

"That isn't true."

"No? Well, what about the others?"

"You're different," he said. "I've told you that."

"Let's talk about Connor Prewitt," Adam said. "He believed you, too. So much so he came out to his ultra-religious family, who disowned him. Did you know he's living out of his car? You should see him. It's very sad."

"No," Dario said. "We lost touch."

"And Shane Brighton? Remember him?"

Dario's posture tensed. "How did you find them?"

"It was easy," he said. "Your wife helped me. She figured I might be able to heal my wounds if I realized I wasn't the only one in this world whose life you tried to take over."

"I did no such thing," Dario said.

"What about Charlie Bower?" Adam asked. The boy's name hung in the air.

Dario leaned forward. The muscles in his jaw tightened. "What did I do to you that was so wrong? Yes, I offered Victor money to leave and urged him to go to Paris without you. But I also covered your medical bills when I heard what had happened. I paid your rent. I took care of your college tuition. I gave your mother the best opportunity in her career. I would do *anything* for you. I don't understand why you're so angry with me, Adam. Maybe this is about *you*. Maybe down deep you know you really want me, but you made a promise to Victor and you're a man of your word."

"I did want you," Adam confessed. "I'm sure you knew that. But you used that against me, Dario."

"It wasn't very difficult to seduce you, Adam. You were more willing than you realize."

"You're good at what you do," he said. "I'll give you that. And God knows you are a beautiful man. But I knew early on I never wanted to be just another plaything to you. I wanted something more."

"More than I can give you?"

"Dario, you can't give me what I want."

"And Victor can?" he asked. "He's a kid. He has nothing."

"But in my eyes, he has everything," Adam said. "Maybe I should be thanking you. Because of what happened between me and you, it helped me realize how lucky I am to have Victor in my life. The more I got to see what your world was like, the less I wanted to be a part of it."

Dario looked wounded, as if Adam had singlehandedly crushed his hopes. "Then why did you come?" he asked. "Why are you here? Because I bought you a ticket and you wanted to see Greece? Because I offered to give you money?"

"We can talk about the money later," he said. "Truth be told, I wanted to see you. I had to."

Dario smiled, relieved. The sparkle of hope returned to his eyes. "There was a part of me that knew you'd be here. I can show you the island later. There's much to see. I'm sure you'll learn to love it here."

He's delusional. You can break it to him in a minute.

"Do you have any idea what happened after you left?" Adam asked. "I mean, do you even care?"

"Of course I do," he said. "I've just been busy."

"Too busy to call your daughter?"

"Her mother is taking care of her."

"Yes, she is," Adam said. "Actually, we all are."

"You're still her tutor?"

"Anastasia doesn't need a tutor anymore," he said. "Not since she finished her first novel and got herself an agent. Have you read the manuscript? It's called *Daddy's Little Boys*. You should probably check it out...since she's dedicating it to you."

If Dario was worried, he didn't let it show. "This book you're talking about...it's real?"

"Apparently, it's a true story," he said. "It's amazing what a twelve-year-old can do these days. The stories they can tell."

"I can stop this book," he said. "You know that. All it takes is one call to my attorney and that novel will never see the light of day."

"And destroy the dreams of your only daughter? Wow. Imagine the sequel."

"You think I'm a bad father?" Dario asked.

"It doesn't really matter what I think about your parenting skills. I think she's much better off actually. You might've done her a favor by walking out of her life."

"I came to Greece because you left," he said. "I couldn't let anyone see I was hurting. What was I supposed to do without you?"

"Looks like you've managed just fine," Adam said. "Suffering on a Greek island on the Aegean Sea? You seem real destroyed."

"You don't think my feelings for you are genuine? Is that it?"

"Where you're concerned, I don't know what's real."

"Then let me show you. Give me a chance to prove to you I'm not this bad person you make me out to be."

"I think you're a monster," Adam said. And his words were true. "You're worse than any person I've ever met. If I had your money and power, maybe I'd be like you. Maybe if I were, I could understand it more. The hiding and the secrets and the lying. Why not just be who you are?"

"It's not as simple as that," he said.

"And it probably never will be for you," said Adam. "I hope you find peace someday, Dario."

"I did," he said. "In you."

"Let's not confuse peace with desire," he said. "Or lust with love."

Dario reached across the table for Adam's hand. "It's just the two of us now," Dario said. "Let's put the past behind us. We can be together. Finally."

Adam pulled his hand away. He knew it was time for him to leave, to say good-bye once and for all. "That's just the thing," he said. "There will never be *us*. There will only be Victor and I."

"He left you, Adam. He went to Paris without you."

"Yes, but he refused your money."

"That was his mistake."

"No," he said. "That was his honor. See, I'm taking the last boat back to Athens. And I'm getting on a plane. I'm flying to Paris."

"And what's in Paris for you?"

"Love," he said. "True love. Something I don't think you'll ever know about."

Dario shook his head. "You're wrong," he said. "I didn't know love until I met you. That day I saw you in your mother's office. You were holding two cans of soda in your hands. And you had that adorable smile on your face. I knew you had to be mine."

"But I never was, Dario," he said. "And I never will be."

"Let me take care of you," said Dario. "If you stay, I'll give you whatever you want. An apartment on the Italian Riviera? A penthouse in Paris? Just name it and I'll buy it."

"That's where you went wrong," he said, "because I've never been for sale."

Dario's dark eyes narrowed. "Everyone has their price."

Adam stood, careful not to bump the top of his head on the ribs of the bright blue umbrella hovering above them. "I've already paid mine," he said. "You know, when I was going back and forth to doctor appointments and all those weeks of physical therapy and getting caught up with homework so I could graduate on time, I kept thinking about you. I wondered where you were and what you were doing and why you weren't with your wife and daughter. I have no doubt Evangelina will be just fine. And I've already told you Anastasia is writing a tell-all, so you might keep an eye out for that. I knew I had to see you. I had to have this moment with you face-to-face, man to man. I needed to see you for who you really are with my own eyes. And now I have."

"You came here to tell me good-bye?" Dario asked.

"I came here to tell you about the money," Adam said. He patted the front pocket of his shorts. "I'm giving it to your wife. Every cent."

"What for?" he said. "She already has enough. She took it from me in the divorce."

"You might not realize this, but many lives have merged because of you," said Adam. "My mother and your wife...I mean, your *ex*-wife…have joined forces. My mother left her job at the bank. She went to work for Evangelina."

Dario locked eyes with Adam. "What are you talking about?"

"Evangelina opened up a free clinic in Chicago. The Lorenzo Maldonado Medical Center. You haven't heard about it?" Adam didn't give Dario the chance to respond. "My mother and Jane and Myrtle Brubaker help Evangelina run the place. They just opened a week ago. They refuse to turn anyone away."

What Adam was telling Dario was only partially true. Yes, most of the money was going to Evangelina's wonderful new project, but some of it was also earmarked for Sheila Harrington, the widow of the man who'd killed himself in the foyer of the Vassalo estate. He'd left not only a wife behind with nothing, but three children as well.

"We won't turn our backs on her," Evangelina had vowed to Becca and Adam. "Not ever. None of this is her fault. Or her children's."

The anger was starting to surface in Dario. Adam could see the tension building in Dario's hands. "Let me guess," Dario said. "You work for my wife, too?"

"No. I'm planning on starting a new life with someone I love more than anyone else in the world."

"And there's nothing I can do to change your mind?"

"During some of my long train rides, I used to imagine what your life was like," Adam said. "The part I never saw. The business side of things. I was so intrigued by you. And when you offered me a glimpse into a world I'd never known before, I took it. It might sound silly to you, but I used to think, I bet he works in a fancy office with real plants and a gorgeous view of the city. And he probably gives all the girls a little pat every now and then so no one suspects anything about him. At Christmas, he gives them all boxes of candy. Truffles, probably. White chocolate or pink champagne. They can't wait to dance with him at the holiday office parties. They shake his hand because they adore him. They worship him like the Greek god he is. Especially the wives. And maybe even a few of the husbands. But he refuses politely because he is a married man. And I can almost hear you saying things to them like, 'Doesn't my wife look lovely tonight?'

"Somewhere along the way, I got angry with you, Dario. When I saw the sadness in your wife's eyes and I read the loneliness in your daughter's words. Then I found out about the others. The young men you lured into your world of secret sex and shame. And then I realized the person I should feel the sympathy for…is you.

"But I refuse to feel sorry for you. And from this moment on, you will never contact me again. Because if you do, I will notify the authorities and ask them to go down to the wine cellar and blow a hole right through the brick wall. You know the part I'm talking about: the section that doesn't look like the rest. Because after Charlie Bower refused you and said no to you, you killed him and you put his body there. You tried to cover it up, but you did a lousy job of it. You're also going to send an anonymous gift to Charlie's family. Money will never bring their son back and give them the peace they want, but at least they'll be taken care of.

"You're trapped, Dario. And you're the only one who can get yourself out. Otherwise, you'll still be that sneaky married man always trying to fool someone and cheat.

"The first time you touched me, I remember thinking, I bet when his beautiful wife comes home from working a long shift at the hospital and she's trying to hug him and kiss him because she missed him so much, it really won't be her he's touching. It won't be her he's kissing or thinking about," Adam said. "It'll be *me*. And I will tell you why… and this is so sad…because you, Dario Vassalo…you are nothing but a coward. And I am nothing to you at all…but a tool for your imagination."

Adam turned.

He walked away.

❖

During the boat ride back to Piraeus, the taxi ride to the airport in Athens, the five-hour wait, and then the early-morning flight to Paris, Adam thought about Victor constantly. He replayed their entire relationship from the moment they'd met in the community college classroom in Chicago up until the present, in which Adam was sitting in a window seat waiting for his first sight of Paris to come into view.

He recalled the very second he saw Victor walk through the classroom door with a backpack strapped to his broad shoulders. Their eyes met. Victor smiled. He sat in the empty chair behind Adam looking nervous and unsure.

It was Adam who spoke first. "I'm sorry to bother you, but do you have a pen I could borrow?"

"Sure."

"Thank you," he said, taking the pen, the first of many. Their fingertips touched but only briefly. Adam looked up and took a second glance into Victor's warm, dark eyes. "What's your name?"

His beautiful mouth bloomed into an adorable smile. "Victor."

"I'm Adam," he said. "It's nice to meet you. I hope you're good at German."

"All the other classes were full," he said. "This was the only one I could get into."

Lucky for me you did.

Soon, the two men found every reason possible to be in each other's presence. It was only when he was with Victor that Adam could escape the haunting memory of his father's death. Even though he'd never met the man, he had plagued Adam's life. He showed up all the time in the constant sorrow in Becca's eyes, in the wave of emotion that crept into his grandfather's voice whenever he reminisced about the youthful days of his son, in the icy edges of Nana's frosty words as every syllable she now spoke came from a place of heartbreak, in the faces of soldiers and sailors and strangers with similar features Adam would bump into on the train or see on television. They made him wonder what his father would be like if he were still alive. Would he acknowledge the obvious love between his son and Victor Maldonado? Would he still love Becca as much as he did when they were eighteen and thought they had forever together?

The plane hit a small patch of turbulence. Adam closed his eyes and flashed back to a series of vivid memories, seeing them like a slide show playing in his mind: their late-night study sessions during which they both butchered the German language, the in-depth and often personal conversations they had while sitting together at sidewalk cafés and in their booth at the Irish pub, their frequent trips to art-house cinemas when occasionally their fingers would intertwine in the dark, sitting in the center of the German village in Lincoln Square where they shared a loaf of bread and some meat and cheese and dreamt about running away to Europe together someday, the drunken afternoon at Oktoberfest and the morning after where they found themselves waking in each other's arms, the soft and hopeful expression on Victor's face when Adam had finally come to his senses and indicated their future together would be a romantic one, the intimate moment they shared on the sofa in Adam's living room when they experienced their first kiss.

Adam licked his lips, recalling the sweet taste of Victor's mouth on his. He couldn't wait until they were alone again and they could take every minute they wanted and needed to explore every inch of each other's bodies. Adam was filled with hot anticipation, anxious for the first time he'd be able to express to Victor physically how much he loved him. He would take his time to show Victor how sensual and gentle he could be. To prove to him why he'd waited to share his first time with Victor.

We have the rest of our lives together. There's no one else in this world I want to spend it with besides him.

Adam felt a strong pang of lust for Victor as the plane began its descent toward a runway at the Aéroport Paris-Charles de Gaulle. It was an intense desire for Victor he'd never allowed himself to experience before. It seemed slightly savage, almost primal, this wild feverish craving to pleasure Victor.

He has no idea what he's gotten himself into, what's in store for him. I can't wait to make him feel as good and loved as he made me feel for the last three years.

The plane landed. He couldn't wait to see that beautiful smile and those gorgeous eyes, to kiss that hot mouth and feel Victor's arms around his body.

I can't wait to start forever with him.

The other passengers couldn't get off the plane fast

enough for Adam. Of course, he was sitting near the back of the plane, only delaying his reunion with Victor even more. Finally, he was able to retrieve his carry-on bag from the overhead compartment. One of the flight attendants mumbled something in French and offered him a not-so-convincing smile as he walked off the plane.

As Adam moved through the airport and followed the signs to baggage claim, he tried to imagine what their new life would be like in Paris. Victor would be busy with classes and sculpting exquisite works of art with his hands. Adam would learn French and find a job working as a copywriter for an ad agency that was looking for young, fresh talent. He would also do all he could to help the Lorenzo Maldonado Medical Center become the great success story of all of their lives. They would spend their evenings together in their apartment, cooking dinner side by side, talking, laughing, and sharing events from their day. They would explore the city on weekends and like all lovers do, find their way to the Eiffel Tower to share a kiss or two while overlooking the world around them. They would go to museums where Victor could share his passion for art by teaching Adam how to appreciate and understand their history, value, and aesthetics.

We're going to fall even deeper in love.

Adam had no regrets where Dario Vassalo was concerned. He knew there was a reason why the older man had entered his life and tempted him with sex and money and power. Yet, deep down, Adam knew those things didn't matter as much to him as the one thing Victor Maldonado could give it to him: love.

I had to meet Dario and experience his world to understand it wasn't for me. It's not who I am, where I come from.

I never want to be someone's secret.

Adam's phone buzzed. It was a text message from Victor. Reading it brought a tremendous smile to Adam's face.

Meet me at carousel 24. I'm waiting for you. I'm the one with the stupid grin on his face.

Adam quickened his step, more anxious than ever. It was only a matter of seconds...

Then it happened.

My God, there he is. He's even more beautiful than I remember.

They moved through the crowd.

These strangers have no idea what this moment means to us. They don't know what we've been through. No one does.

Adam felt his eyes fill with tears and a powerful wave of emotion surge through his body.

They reached each other and slid into each other's arms to create the perfect fit.

"My God, I love you," Victor breathed.

Their mouths met briefly. They sealed their future with a kiss.

"I'm sorry it took me so long to get to you," Adam said. He looked deep into Victor's eyes.

"Believe me, Adam Parsh," he said. "You were definitely worth the wait."

Adam reached up and brushed away the tears of joy on Victor's cheeks. "Promise me...we will never be apart again," he said.

Victor reached for both of Adam's hands and placed them in his own. "You have my word," he said.

Adam smiled. Already he wanted to kiss Victor again. "What do we do now?" he asked.

Victor reached for Adam's carry-on bag. "Something I've wanted us to do from the very beginning," he said. "Let's go home, Adam. To *our* home."

Adam couldn't help himself. He leaned in and kissed Victor's lips once more. "You'll have to show me the way," he said.

"It will be my pleasure," said Victor.

They started to move toward an exit, to the world outside that was waiting to become theirs.

Adam stopped. Victor did the same. "Victor, do you know what it feels like inside my heart right now? Being here...and all the love I have for you? How can we even describe this?"

Their eyes met and locked when Victor spoke. "This is forever," he said. "And that is something that will *never* change."

About the Author

A California native, Dylan Madrid grew up in the Bay Area. He opted to backpack through seven countries before heading to college and spent a year living in Europe, primarily on the Greek island of Ios. When he's not dreaming about living on the Italian Riviera or running away to Belgium, Dylan teaches college courses in writing and the arts.

Books Available From Bold Strokes Books

Lake Thirteen by Greg Herren. A visit to an old cemetery seems like fun to a group of five teenagers, who soon learn that sometimes it's best to leave old ghosts alone. (978-1-60282-894-0)

Deadly Cult by Joel Gomez-Dossi. One nation under MY God, or you die. (978-1-60282-895-7)

The Case of the Rising Star: A Derrick Steele Mystery by Zavo. Derrick Steele's next case involves blackmail, revenge, and a new romance as Derrick races to save a young movie star from a dangerous killer. Meanwhile, will a new threat from within destroy him, along with the entire Steele family? (978-1-60282-888-9)

Big Bad Wolf by Logan Zachary. After a wolf attack, Paavo Wolfe begins to suspect one of the victims is turning into a werewolf. Things become hairy as his ex-partner helps him find the killer. Can Paavo solve the mystery before he runs into the Big Bad Wolf? (978-1-60282-890-2)

The Plain of Bitter Honey by Alan Chin. Trapped within the bleak prospect of a society in chaos, twin brothers Aaron and Hayden Swann discover inner strength in the face of tragedy and search for atonement after betraying the one you most love. (978-1-60282-883-4)

In His Secret Life by Mel Bossa. The only man Allan wants is the one he can't have. (978-1-60282-875-9)

The Moon's Deep Circle by David Holly. Tip Trencher wants to find out what happened to his long-lost brothers, but what he finds is a sizzling circle of gay sex and pagan ritual. (978-1-60282-870-4)

Straight Boy Roommate by Kevin Troughton. Tom isn't expecting much from his first term at University, but a chance encounter with straight boy Dan catapults him into an extraordinary, wild weekend of sex and self-discovery, which turns his life upside down, and leads him into his first love affair. (978-1-60282-782-0)

Raising Hell: Demonic Gay Erotica, edited by Todd Gregory. Hot stories of gay erotica featuring demons. (978-1-60282-768-4)

Pursued by Joel Gomez-Dossi. Openly gay college student Jamie Bradford becomes romantically involved with two men at the same time, and his hell begins when one of his boyfriends becomes intent on killing him. (978-1-60282-769-1)

Timothy by Greg Herren. Timothy is a romantic suspense thriller from award-winning mystery writer Greg Herren set in the fabulous Hamptons. (978-1-60282-760-8)

In Stone by Jeremy Jordan King. A young New Yorker is rescued from a hate crime by a mysterious someone who turns out to be more of a something. (978-1-60282-761-5)

The Jesus Injection by Eric Andrews-Katz. Murderous statues, demented drag queens, political bombings, ex-gay ministries, espionage, and romance are all in a day's work for a top secret agent. But the gloves are off when Agent Buck 98 comes up against the Jesus Injection. (978-1-60282-762-2)

Combustion by Daniel W. Kelly. Bearish detective Deck Waxer comes to the city of Kremfort Cove to investigate why the hottest men in town are bursting into flames in broad daylight. (978-1-60282-763-9)

Night Shadows: Queer Horror edited by Greg Herren and J.M. Redmann. *Night Shadows* features delightfully wicked stories by some of the biggest names in queer publishing. (978-1-60282-751-6)

Wyatt: Doc Holliday's Account of an Intimate Friendship by Dale Chase. Erotica writer Dale Chase takes the remarkable friendship between Wyatt Earp, upright lawman, and Doc Holliday, Southern gentlemen turned gambler and killer, to an entirely new level: hot! (978-1-60282-755-4)

Secret Societies by William Holden. An outcast hustler, his unlikely "mother," his faithless lovers, and his religious persecutors—all in 1726. (978-1-60282-752-3)

The Jetsetters by David-Matthew Barnes. As rock band the Jetsetters skyrocket from obscurity to superstardom, Justin Holt, a lonely barista, and Diego Delgado, the band's guitarist, fight with everything they have to stay together, despite the chaos and fame. (978-1-60282-745-5)

Strange Bedfellows by Rob Byrnes. Partners in life and crime, Grant Lambert and Chase LaMarca are hired to make a politician's compromising photo disappear, but what should be an easy job quickly spins out of control. (978-1-60282-746-2)

Fontana by Joshua Martino. Fame, obsession, and vengeance collide in a novel that asks: What if America's greatest hero was gay? (978-1-60282-675-5)

The Dirty Diner: Gay Erotica on the Menu, edited by Jerry L. Wheeler. Gay erotica set in restaurants, featuring food, sex, and men—could you really ask for anything more? (978-1-60282-677-9)

Sweat: Gay Jock Erotica by Todd Gregory. Sizzling tales of smoking-hot sex with the athletic studs everyone fantasizes about. (978-1-60282-669-4)

The Marrying Kind by Ken O'Neill. Just when successful wedding planner Adam More decides to protest inequality by quitting the business and boycotting marriage entirely, his only sibling announces her engagement. (978-1-60282-670-0)